ALTHYN

AND THE

OTHIAN DAGGER

ANASTASIA RABIYAH

PURPLE SWORD PUBLICATIONS
www.PurpleSword.com

All rights reserved. No part of this book may be reproduced in any form or by any electronic means, including information storage and retrieval systems, without permission in writing from the publisher, except by a reviewer who may quote brief passages in review.

This is a work of fiction. Names, places, characters, and events are fictitious in every regard. Any similarities to actual events and persons, living or dead, is purely coincidental. Any trademarks, service marks, product names, or named features are assumed to be the property of their respective owners, and are used only for reference. There is no implied endorsement if any of these terms are used.

ALTHYN AND THE OTHIAN DAGGER
Copyright © 2010 ANASTASIA RABIYAH. All rights reserved worldwide.
ISBN 978-1-936165-47-6
Cover Art Designed By Anastasia Rabiyah
Photographs Copyright Leafsomen, Spectral-design, Luxora, Dreamstime.com
Edited By Brieanna Robertson and D. Thomas Jerlo
Published by Purple Sword Publications, LLC
www.PurpleSword.com

ALTHYN

AND THE

OTHIAN DAGGER

Foreword

"Storyweavers will spin you tales about the mer, fabulous tellings of fantasy, of beautiful creatures that reside beneath the depths to lure sailors to their deaths. They will tell you that the mer are born of the surf, from froth and bubbles brought across the wet sand by the tide. They will tell you the mer are mystical and magical and that our womankind can love the men that walk the land. What do they know? How can they see the cold depth of our hearts, or guess at the violent ways in which we assert our rank? The storyweavers weave naught but fanciful lies."

–Althyn Laethwyn

Dedication:

For Ashley Netten, forever my evil sis,
the person responsible for bringing out this dark muse.

"*As there is a use in medicine for poisons,*
so the world cannot move without rogues."
-Ralph Waldo Emerson

"*A villain must be a thing of power, handled with delicacy and grace. He must be wicked enough to excite our aversion, strong enough to arouse our fear, human enough to awaken some transient gleam of sympathy. We must triumph in his downfall, yet not barbarously nor with contempt, and the close of his career must be in harmony with all its previous development.*"
-Agnes Repplier

Chapter One
The Island

SHE MOVED AS the waves, with grace and rhythm, neither a creature wholly of the land, nor of the sea by which she had grown up. Althyn stopped and stood beside the ramshackle dock, watching her father's ship approach. It was a great, gilded vessel with pale sails and a dark flag that flapped and billowed from the highest mast. She was only nineteen summers and looked much like her mother. Long, blonde locks whipped about her face to obscure her father's arrival. She didn't look forward to her father's visits, but rather hoped her uncle Anthis would be along, for she loved his stories of the Othian Church's wonders, the riches the outside world bore, and his kind attention, which was so unlike her father's cruelty.

The ship sidled to the old dock, dropped anchor, and sure enough, Uncle Anthis's lanky body appeared as he threw the ropes over the side. Althyn ran along the wood, her bare feet making little sound, the weight of her blonde hair, uncut since birth, bouncing at her back. She knew Anthis would bring her fine gifts, silks from far off places she doubted she'd ever be allowed to visit.

After catching up the end of the rope he had tossed, she tied it off and waited, impatient. The plank lowered and thumped into place. Althyn resisted running up to embrace her uncle. She often wondered why he had received the ill end of the bargain with his looks when her father had acquired handsomeness that hid his brutality. *Maybe they were not of the same father*, she reasoned.

Her father strode down first, glanced at her in an appraising moment of disapproval, said not a word, and went on his way as he always did, in a state of dazed obsession. She turned and watched him leave, his figure tall, dark, and imposing. He bore a scar on his left cheek that she'd always wanted to ask about, but she feared him too much to do so. The enormous battleaxe he carried was strapped to his back, as always.

"How's my lass?" Anthis called. Behind him on the ship, the crew muddled about, too afraid to step foot on the deserted island. She knew her father had warned them not to. His visits came and went in the same manner each month. Never had she been allowed to speak to the others, though she spied at them from her vantage, and wondered if they were like her father, or like her uncle in manner.

She sighed happily and held her arms out to Anthis. He stood a head taller than her and still, as he'd been doing since she was a child, he picked her up and swung her around three times.

"You've grown," he said, his brown eyes flickering up and down her threadbare, white dress. "Good thing you and your mother stay here." He licked his lips and smiled a crooked grin.

"Why, Uncle?" She clasped his gnarled hand, their fingers intertwining for the walk back to the cottage.

"Where I'm from, all the men and elves would stare at you. They'd not be able to deny you a thing. Althyn, aside from your mother, you're the most beautiful woman I've ever seen."

She blushed and lowered her gaze to the beach. The warm, wet sand crinkled between her toes. Side by side, they ambled along. She kept the pace slow, unwilling to arrive home too soon after her father. He'd want time alone with her mother.

"Did you bring me anything?" She squeezed his long fingers.

Anthis stopped. He lifted her chin with his free hand and chuckled. "Of course I have. Treasures to dress in and combs for your hair."

She smiled. "I wish *you* were my father." She didn't care that he was ugly or ill-mannered. Althyn liked the way he looked at her and the fact that he noticed her at all. "You would stay with us if you were. You wouldn't leave like Papa does."

Sucking in a startled breath, Anthis looked away, on up the path to where they must go soon enough. "It wasn't in the stars for me to have a wife. You see me. I am no trophy, nothing a woman would desire. But yes…if your mother could love me, I would never leave her side. She loves my brother, Arin, and always has. There is no changing that truth."

Her chest heaved with excitement. *If only I can convince her to be with him. She'll grow to love him as I do. She'll see. He would never hurt her, never.* Althyn tugged her uncle along. They half-ran up the path. Her mother's cottage stood at the crest of a hill surrounded by jungle trees and a little barn to one side where they kept three goats and a mule. She kept another treasure in there, a baby gryphon she'd found by the southern crags, fallen from its nest. It couldn't fly yet, too young and too weak to do so.

The door swung open in the wind, the hinges creaking. Even at a distance, Althyn heard her mother's screams, her father's leering laughter. They were making love, rutting like wild beasts, most likely on the rug in the main room. She didn't understand her mother's infatuation with her father. He was vile. His temper flared like a wildfire, and he beat her mother when they argued because he grew impatient with her pleas to live with him on the island of his birth.

"I don't want to go home yet," she told her uncle. "Come see my pet."

"Pet?" His bushy eyebrows knitted. A wisp of his oily, black hair fell across his face.

She pushed it behind his pointed ear, the one trait she seemed to share with her father's race. "Oh yes, my new pet. She's pure white. When she grows enough, I'll train her, and she'll let me on her back. She'll fly me from this island and out into the world to see all the wonders you speak of."

Anthis shifted from boot to boot, uncomfortable. "You should stay here. It's safer for you here."

She sighed, discouraged. "Come see her."

Relenting, he followed her into the dim light of the barn. It smelled like fresh hay and the oily fur of goats. There was another scent, spicy and foreign, one that set Althyn at ease and made her feel like she belonged to something larger than the deserted island and her father's control. It was the musky odor of the gryphon's feathers.

The creature burbled when she entered its stall.

Behind her, Anthis gasped. "By the three sisters, do you know how much that thing's blood sells for? Even its feathers? The sorcerers in Delnaith would pay through the nose for it."

Althyn shrugged. She knelt down beside the gryphon and stroked its feathered head. "She likes me."

Anthis cleared his throat. "Girl, don't let your father know about this. He'll...well, you can imagine, I'm sure."

She nodded, well aware of his unpredictable wrath and his greed.

Her uncle reached out with quivering fingers and stroked the gryphon's head. The animal made a purring sound, her golden eyes widening. She stretched her back and flicked her tufted tail.

"She likes you, too," Althyn said, pleased.

They lingered for a time, discussing Anthis's latest adventure in the world. "We traveled all the way to the Othian Church, took one of their leader's slaves and gold and riches beyond belief." He stared at the ground a moment. "But we didn't find the Othian Dagger, the one thing your father wanted from that backwards place."

"Why does he want it?"

Anthis shook his head. "I know naught why your father collects what he does. He has his own plans, and I follow as I've always done, as a younger brother should."

"It sounds like a wonderful life. I wish someday that I could go with you." As always, he discouraged such hopes, but no matter what he told her, she believed the lands across the sea were places of wonder. No amount of tavern tales or dreary stories of being lost in forests near where their marks were swayed her into believing that the little, deserted isle she'd inhabited all her life was paradise.

Trudging back to the cottage, Althyn heard her mother's high-pitched cries of terror, not the same peels of pain from earlier. She shot Anthis a horrified look and sprinted along the flowerbed. Thick thuds reverberated within the little home. Behind her, Anthis called for her to stop, but she couldn't, not until she knew her mother was safe. She ran through the open doorway.

Her mother lay in a heap beside the hearth, her blonde hair streaked with blood, her green eyes wide with fear. She never looked over, her gaze trained on Althyn's father. He stood above her with his fist raised.

"Stop," Althyn whispered, feeling helpless and insignificant.

Neither heard her, or if they did, they didn't make a move to show it.

Her father took a step forth and swung. His fist crushed into soft cheek and bone. Althyn shrieked when her mother's petite body jolted in the opposite direction. She crashed into the water buckets, knocking them across the floor. She knew there would be hours of singing and rocking with her later to right the wrongs her father had done this day.

"Stop!" Althyn took her first step inside. Her eyes narrowed; her jaw tightened so hard that it hurt.

Her father turned, a feral look on his face. Before this day, a mere glance from him had made her cower, but not now. She'd had enough of his cruelty. Someone needed to put a stop to this, and her uncle never tried.

"Leave her alone," she squeaked out.

He came for her. She knew what to expect. Althyn balled her hands into fists, but she wouldn't fight. The object was to draw his attention from her mother. Her father's first blow sent her careening outside. She fell hard against the path, her cheek throbbing from his fist.

"Stay out of this," he spoke low, his upper lip curling, stretching the scar on his cheek. "You little whore. You're no better than she is." He crossed the threshold, bent over, and grasped her thin dress. It tore as he lifted her.

"Stop," she pleaded. "Don't do this."

Behind her, she heard her uncle approach, his boots crunching on the seashell path. He would watch, helpless, as he always did. Uncle Anthis, despite his love, was no match for his brother.

Her father didn't stop. He never did until he'd beaten her into submission, just as he did to her mother. Slap after slap bit into her face. She closed her eyes and clenched her teeth, fighting the cries of pain that quelled in her throat. Finally, he tossed her aside, satisfied.

Althyn lay still as death across the yellow flowers her mother had planted. She tried not to breathe, not to think, not to do anything that would draw his attention now.

"I'm going hunting," he said with a growl. And then, he was gone.

Anthis lifted Althyn and carried her inside. He set her on the bench by the window where she did nothing but stare at her mother's prone form. Both women's clothing was torn, her mother's spotted with crimson. Uncle Anthis shut the front door and clumsily set things to right.

"Yneria?" he asked when he'd finished cleaning up the mess. "Can you hear me?" He knelt beside her mother and lifted her head into his lap. With a tender touch, he stroked her forehead, pain in his sparkling, brown eyes. "Can I get you something? Some water?"

She moaned. Her eyes flickered like a dying flame. "He'll kill me soon. I feel it coming." She reached up and tried to push Anthis's loose hair away from his face, but failed. "I am tired. Some nights, I long for this to end. It was a mistake to choose him, a mistake I have suffered ever since."

"Uncle, please," Althyn begged. She needed to see the rest of the world, to find the cities over the seas and discover all the riches her uncle told her of. She needed her mother to leave her father, and there was no one else she knew that could help but him. "Take us from here."

Her mother held her palm up, her denial of the request. "My place is at his side." Even after he'd beaten her down, she still professed her loyalty.

"How can you love him, Mama?"

"One day you will understand. Our kind take one mate…for life. I pray you make a good choice." Her mother shook her head. "Anthis, there is something I need you to know about me...and about my daughter. She's growing, changing...will soon feel the weight of what she is."

Her uncle glanced over his shoulder at Althyn, one black eyebrow upraised with curiosity. He frowned and returned his attentions to her mother. "What is it, Yneria?"

"I am not elfin-kind or human. I took this shape to please him. Althyn is only half elf from her father's blood...and half mer." Her sea-green eyes slipped shut; her lips trembled. "When my daughter comes of age, which will be soon after my death, you must return her to the sea. There, my people will welcome her. She has no place among the land-walkers."

Anthis nodded and held his silence.

Appalled, Althyn stood and turned her back on them. She walked as steadily as she could straight out of the cottage. All her life she'd known she was different, but not how or why. The sea called to her at times with such intensity that she wanted to throw herself into its watery arms. This explained it.

She trudged into the barn, opened the gryphon's stall, and curled up beside the sleeping animal. She imagined the creature was her baby sister, a being sent for her to care for and bond with, her own animalistic angel.

As she lay among the hay and willed her wounds to heal, she wondered how long it would take for the gryphon to grow large enough to carry her away. Now that she knew what her other half was, she wondered what would happen if she slipped into the waves. *What wonders await me in the cold depths? Has my escape been at the shore all this time?*

Chapter Two
White Sister

THE COOL, EVENING wind poured off the sea and through the single window in the barn. Althyn was not quite asleep when she heard her father coming. He opened the barn door with such force that it crashed against the wall outside. She held still, waiting and hoping he'd not notice her. The gryphon stirred and clicked its beak, its golden, catlike eyes blinking. Her father's boots loudly crushed the fresh hay. She heard his heavy breathing. The spicy scent of his skin and the leather vest he favored made her nostrils flare.

Her father clucked his tongue.

Althyn looked up and frowned.

He hung over the stall, one eyebrow raised as he stared at the gryphon. "What's that?" he whispered. His voiceless tone always frightened her. "You're hugging it. A nasty little thing it is, too." He swung the stall door and reached down with one, cruel hand, snatching the gryphon up by the neck.

The startled creature squawked and thrashed.

As if he were prepping a chicken for the pot, he tore out its wing feathers methodically.

"No!" she shouted, stumbling as she got to her feet. "Don't!"

He tossed the bloodstained quills at her face. Talons clawed and scratched into his skin, but he didn't react. With a sickening crack, her father snapped one wing, breaking it.

The gryphon wailed and struggled.

Crack.

Althyn wanted to kill him. She wanted to tear him apart more than she wanted to escape the island, more than anything she had ever wanted. Yet, she stood there, helpless against his cruelty. Her eyes remained fixed on his face as he crushed the gryphon's neck between his long fingers and twisted its head to the side. He threw the body at her feet.

"Let that be a lesson to you." He sneered and spun, crunching in the hay back the way he'd come. No doubt he'd seek out her mother once more. The beating would continue.

Althyn sank to her knees. She picked up a single wing feather and ran its length across her lips. *Soft.* The broken body bled into the hay. The pure, pale feathers were stained with sanguine blood now, ruined. *He destroys everything.* She envied his power, his coldness. *If I were so cruel, no one could hurt me like he does.*

She gathered the gryphon against her chest and cried, swearing it would be the last time tears fell from her eyes. When her sorrow ran its course and she was able to catch her breath, she carried the dead animal outside, took up a striker and piled hay over its body. Althyn burned her *sister's* body and pursed her lips, plotting revenge.

The smoke trailed up to the stars, blotting some out with inky tendrils. Althyn pushed off the remainder of her ruined dress. She tossed the cloth on the fire, turned her back on the empty feeling in her heart, and started for the sea.

Wild grass tickled her ankles as she ambled down the hill. The waves called to her as they always did, singing in shushing whispers, luring her closer. She wanted to get lost in there for a time, to understand why her mother had left it for this terrible life.

Loam gave way to smooth, round rocks beneath her bare feet. The rocks gave way to sand. Waves slapped and crashed into the shore. Her feet met the icy water, the popping foam, and pull of tides. Althyn stepped into the sea and moved until the water covered her body. She floated for a time, the cold not bothering her in the least. In fact, it comforted her, made her feel whole and strong. She rolled over and dipped beneath the surface to swim down into the darkness.

Her eyes adjusted to the sea and the change of light. Silver fish darted past her, flicking fins and staring at her with round, unblinking eyes. Althyn's legs itched. She kicked and arched her back to glide along. *I wish I could swim as they do.* The itching grew worse until it burned. She glanced back and felt change come over her body. Her skin crawled and tingled. Bits sloughed off into the water, staining it even in the gray light shining from a moon high above. Bones moved and melded. Her legs fused into one powerful appendage, a scaled tail that whipped and curled. Wide fins grew from the end, and one feathery wisp of a fin trailed at its center, spreading wide and undulating.

All alone and transformed, Althyn smiled at this newfound secret. She curved her body and gave a swift flick of her tail. Propelled forward, she lost her balance and dipped toward the coral. She splayed her arms and righted her course. Swimming in this new hiding place, she contemplated her future. Breathing in the water was as sweet if not more so as breathing in air. *I'm free,* she realized. *Free to go anywhere, do anything I wish. Who can stop me now? I will always have this haven to return to – a place I truly belong.* The thought empowered her. Althyn decided it was time for change in her life.

She turned round and headed for the shore. As she approached the beach, she willed her tail to diminish and her legs to return. Glimmering scales peeled away from her skin and floated into the water like lost coins. Her toes wiggled as they emerged. Fins tore away and the taste of blood rent the depths. Althyn licked her lips, savoring it. Blood brought forth a new hunger and reminded her of her *sister* and the droplets of red that had pooled on the dead gryphon's shining feathers. *I will have my revenge.*

She emerged from the sea and padded along the shore, seeking the hill that led to the cottage. Finding her way, she ascended through sand, stone, and grass to exact her vengeance. The wind stirred and moved. High above, clouds rolled in from the east and the first moon hid behind them, as if she were unwilling to see what might happen next.

Althyn strode along the path, the smooth caps of the clamshells cushioning her way. She reached for the handle, feeling ready. When she opened it and saw her uncle lying across the floor where her mother had been earlier, she froze. The vigor she'd felt when she shifted her shape vanished. The hearth held no flames. The windows were busted out. Althyn hurried to Anthis's side and bent down to touch his face. He breathed. A blue bruise stood out on his forehead.

"Uncle?"

He muttered in his unconsciousness, babbling and blubbering incoherencies. Althyn stood and breathed deeply, trying to regain her earlier courage. It was not like her father to take her mother from the cottage. On his haphazard visits, his course remained steady. He arrived, they mated, he beat her down, and he left.

She stepped back outside and closed her eyes to listen. The sea whispered its usual tales. The wind caressed her nude body. The trees in the jungle waved their thick leaves. Far off, just beyond recognition, she heard it. A guttural cry that belied defeat. Her mother's earlier prophecy might well be coming to pass at that moment.

Althyn's heart pounded. She opened her eyes and started at a clumsy run toward the jungle. Darkness and shadows swallowed her fair form as she gained grace and sprinted at top speed toward the clearing by the river. Her muscles tensed and stretched, and she felt more alive than she ever had.

Something thunked and thunked once more, a vicious sound, wet and violent. The moon came peeking down from the heavens and lit the ghostly scene. Her father raised his axe and swung. Her mother's body lay in pieces as he mutilated her remains.

She wanted to scream, to wail, but as before with the gryphon, she merely stood there, helpless. It was already too late. Althyn witnessed the destruction of her mother. She stared, blank and lost as he rent apart her limbs and hacked and swung until there was little left but blood and gore.

He stopped and set his axe to one side, leaning on it like a cane. A strange look crossed his face as he turned. He stared right at her, his eyes narrowed and the moonlight catching on the scar across his cheek. Althyn realized she didn't want to know anything else about her father.

She breathed deep and took the first step. All around her, the breeze surged and gathered. A drop of rain pattered on her shoulder then slid down her breast to fall away. Her hair swirled and eddied in the strengthening wind. Her father raised his axe and shook off the blood.

"You will not hurt me again," Althyn called. Her voice sounded like music, lilting and dangerous as it echoed oddly in the jungle. Lightning crackled overhead, and thunder boomed just behind. Her body tensed with a charge, a power she had not known before. She raised one hand and pointed at him.

Her father glared and spat as he spoke, "I'll kill you too this night and be done with her trickery. All this time I wondered how she kept me ensnared, why I was driven to return to this place and couple with her. I had all I wanted before she captured me…all I needed…"

Lightning cracked and touched down mere inches from her father's boots. His hair stood on end and his eyes widened for a bare moment, then narrowed to the cruel visage she'd always known. *He never loved me…or my mother for that matter. Perhaps my mother had seen that as a challenge, a goal to meet that she never did.*

"Come here, you little whore. It's time you go the way your mother went. I'll have no daughter of mine out in the world controlling men as your mother did me!" He lunged forth, axe rising, readying.

Althyn raced to meet him. Rain pounded down in a torrent, splashing up from the thick loam, powdering her pale skin and giving her courage. *I am not alone. The element hears me. It answers.* The wind beat at her father, and she barreled straight into his chest, reaching for his axe. Her fingers gripped its handle. She clenched tight.

Caught off guard, he fell backward. Leaves crushed and slapped around him. Wet from the blood and rain, the handle of his battleaxe slipped free as she wrenched it to herself. Althyn raised it high, her eyes dangerous slits as she glared one last time at him. *No man will control me as he did…never.* "Your soul will reside in this weapon for all time! Suffer each day without the release of true death."

She swung and hit her mark, cleaving his head off. His face disappeared into the foliage, never to leer at her again. She walked round the body and surveyed it, a warm feeling of sick pleasure rising in her chest. She swung, and his right arm broke free. Then his left…his legs, his chest. She destroyed him as he'd done to her mother, and she felt nothing as she did it except for a faint hatred that burned deep.

Althyn turned her back on her parents and carried the bloodied weapon like a newborn babe in her arms. Rain washed away the death as she passed through the thick grass toward the cottage. It wasn't home to her now, the island, the shore, none of it. She ran the pad of her thumb across the axe's handle and chuckled. "Do you hate it in there, Father?"

No one answered.

She felt his soul though, trapped and afraid, imprisoned for all time. Althyn entered the cottage and sat upon the bench to wait for her uncle to wake. She stared at him, biding her time, and making her plan to begin her new life and see the outside world.

Chapter Three
A New Tide

ANTHIS DID NOT wake until the morning. When he did, he began to cry. He curled his knees to his chest and muttered, over and over, "It's my fault."

Althyn studied her uncle, seeing him in a different light this new day. She no longer felt helpless about her future or her life. Her mother and father were dead, and she could go any which way she chose. "Sit up, and dry your eyes," she said, but her voice held no soothing tone. "By right, my father's ship is mine now. The crew belongs to me."

"Wh-wh-what?" Her uncle wiped his nose across his black shirt, leaving a slick line of snot to shine there. His stringy hair hung in his eyes. "What do you mean?"

"My father is dead. I killed him." She held up the battle axe, a fierce feeling of pride swelling her chest. "All that he owned is mine now. Mine!" She shook the axe once and pursed her lips.

Anthis swallowed hard, his throat clicking and his eyes wide. "Child, what have you done? Where are your clothes? What...what are you saying?" He stumbled when he stood and held to the hearth for support.

"He killed my mother!" Tears burned in her eyes. She held them back, stubborn. "So I killed him in the same fashion."

"By the three sisters," Anthis mumbled. He turned his back on her and lurched to the table to pour a mug of water. "This cannot be."

"Gather yourself. We leave this island today. I will not come back." She stood and carried the axe with her through the main room and down the short hall to her mother's chamber. There, at the foot of the bed, sat an ancient chest, one she'd always wanted to open, but out of respect of her mother's privacy, she had not.

With nimble fingers, she pried the latch and lifted the lid. Fine silken dresses hid the treasure beneath. Althyn pushed them aside. She stared down at what waited for her. A long sword, far too gangly to be wielded, rested there, its hilt fashioned with silver mermaids encrusted with glittering gems. She dropped her father's axe and reached for the sword with both hands. Surprisingly, it bore little weight. "Probably magicked to be light," she whispered. "What a fine treasure this is for me. A sword, bold and brilliant. A weapon to be reckoned with."

She decided at that moment that she favored weapons, tools for bringing about death and change. Althyn swung once and grinned. "This sword is mine." Satisfied, she placed it back in the chest and set the axe within. She chose one of the dresses, an embroidered garment of purple too fine to wear on a deserted island, too fine, in fact, to wear outdoors at all. She didn't care. *I can do whatever I wish.*

Dressed and ready, she returned to the main room and nodded at her uncle. "Go and tell the crew to come round to the cottage and fetch my things. I want the bed brought onto the ship. I want a room set up just for me with fineries and fabrics to make it a woman's place. Bring the chest, the items of value. After it's all loaded, see that this cottage is burned to the ground.

Anthis raised a hand to argue. "They will not follow a woman."

Her eyes narrowed on him. "They will or I'll kill each and every one." She flicked her wrist as if shooing an insect. "I don't need them."

Gasping, Anthis shook his head. "Althyn, you cannot sail your father's ship without a crew. It's impossible. Even the two of us could do no such thing."

"I can do whatever I want," she said, her voice a low grumble. "Don't doubt me, Uncle. Not now, not ever." She turned her back on him in a swirl of fabric and padded, still barefoot, toward the door. Glancing over her shoulder, her upper lip curled. "I killed my father, and I'll do the same to anyone that defies me."

Anthis nodded.

She left him, slamming the door to assert her meaning. Althyn strode to the crest of the hill beside the barn and looked out over the sea, roiling and churning below. It whispered to her of secrets and stories and promised her a haven of silence. She shook her head. "Not yet. I've no wish to hide there. I will have what my father always sought and never found. I will have the dagger of Othia."

A high wave crashed against the beach, white froth sliding back in its wake. She wondered where the others of her kind were. *Why have I never seen them?* The wind picked up off the sea, and she smelled the salt infused in it. Althyn breathed deeply. Her hair fluttered behind her in loose tendrils. She stood there inspecting the crew while they trudged up from the docks to do her bidding.

They grumbled under their breath. Even though she stood a fair distance away, she heard each suspicious word and caught the blatant stares. They looked at her in a way she had not known. Sure, her uncle gave her that same stare, but these elves did so with intensity. She felt the heat of their gazes crossing the shape of her body, taking in her curves. Some watched her with longing, others with an expression she recognized from her father. He used to glare at her mother like that. The crew looked on her with lust.

"Lust," she whispered, a devilish grin curving her lips. "Yes. Let them look. Let them stare." She raised her chin as she watched each elf haul off a piece of her past, balancing chairs or wooden boxes across their broad shoulders. One of the crew stood out to her, a tanned one with black, curly hair framing a square face. He did not glance her way at all. By the shape of his ears, he was human. He wore black pants and laced sandals that tapped when he walked. It was this one that carried her mother's chest down the path. As he ascended, she took in his backside, her breath catching. This one was nice to look upon.

Soon, flames lapped at the sod roof of her mother's house. Acrid, black smoke plumed and pummeled the wind on its way to the sky. Midday saw the end of Althyn's former life. She set her back to the blaze and to the high hill where she'd been born and lived her nineteen summers. Crossing the path for the last time, she kept her gaze on *her* ship, its sails already drawn and the plank awaiting its last passenger.

She strode up the wood, feeling its dampness against the soles of her feet. The flag raised high. She shook her head. "No!" Althyn shouted, her voice carrying across the deck. "Fold that and stow it below. I will raise a new flag, a symbol that reflects my ownership." She paused at the bow and weighed each man's worth.

Her uncle stood near the cabin, an unmistakable smirk of amusement on his thin lips. His oily hair blew around his narrow face. Dressed in black, as he usually did, Althyn thought he looked decidedly grim there in the shadows.

She stood tall, squaring her shoulders and glaring back at all those that watched. "My name is Althyn," she began, and the wind carried her voice with an unsettling clarity. "Althyn Laethwyn. I am Arin's daughter. He's dead. Killed by my hand and deserving of it. If any of you cross me, I'll kill you, too." Her speech complete, she bypassed the majority of the crew, waved one fair hand, and ordered, "Set sail for the mainland, for Truias."

Though none argued with her or dared to say anything at all, one elf glared, his mouth a twisted line of disgust. Black hair framed his face, and he tapped a dagger strapped in his belt with unsaid meaning.

"Uncle, I will go to my room now." She eyed the elf before turning to Anthis.

Her uncle nodded. "It's the one at the end of the hall below. The door is open. I hope you find it to your liking." He glanced over the crew, clearly troubled, but hiding it as best he could. The men began to shuffle to their duties.

Althyn opened the cabin door, winked at her uncle, and started down the steps to inspect her new quarters. She knew, even then, it was only a matter of time before the crew tested her leadership.

Her uncle followed, his boots thumping on the wood. "My lass, you'll need shoes. The wood will give you splinters if you're not careful."

She paused in the hall and lifted her skirt to examine her feet. "I've never worn shoes." She glanced up at him. "I want ones like the black-haired human. Open ones that lace up my calf and allow my skin air."

Anthis chuckled at her. "I will tell him to make you a pair." He leaned against the wall and regarded her for a time. "I'm sorry about Yner—your mother. I feel responsible."

Althyn stared straight into his dark eyes. "It was not your fault, Uncle. She chose her fate when she chose my father."

He looked away and picked at the wood with his jagged nail. "I didn't have the courage to fight him sooner. He's always led me...and I have always followed."

"You will follow me now." She reached across and patted his shoulder.

He flinched at her touch. When he met her gaze, she saw the fear in his eyes. A surge of dominance spread through her, and she decided she liked that look, even from her uncle, the only man she trusted.

"Yes, I will do all that you ask of me." He made a small bow and took his leave.

"Uncle?" she called. When he turned, she went on. "Send the human to my room to make me shoes now."

"As you wish," Anthis whispered, his eyes widening for an instant. He swallowed hard and climbed the steps to the deck.

Althyn felt the ship swaying in the tides. They were on the move, venturing away from her beginning to adventures and treasures yet to be found. She opened the door to her room and entered, her eyes flickering over each object. The bed had been mounted to the floor and draped with silks. A stack of fine, beaded pillows graced the head. A purple velvet coverlet met her curious fingers. "Perfect," she whispered.

She seated herself on the foot of the bed and stared straight ahead at the mysterious trinket hanging on the wall before her. It appeared to be a painting, its surface like polished silver and its frame gilded and carved with flowers. The woman in the portrait reminded her of her mother only she was more beautiful, her face heart-shaped and narrow, her red lips round and ripe. She wore a dark purple dress and her honey-colored hair draped over her shoulders.

Althyn frowned.

The woman frowned.

Althyn reached up to trace her lips, and the woman in the portrait mimicked her. She stood up and crossed the room. Touching the cold glass, she realized what it was. "Like a reflecting pool of water without the ripples." She pushed her wild hair from her face and grinned. "I *am* beautiful." She found her mother's comb and sat before the mirror, staring in wonder at her face. With slow strokes, she brushed out her tresses and braided them in a fanciful way, taken by her striking visage.

Out in the hall, tapping footsteps sounded. She didn't turn, but continued to groom herself. A knock rapped on her door.

"What is it?" she grumbled, angry at being interrupted.

A low voice answered. "Lainious. Your uncle said you have need of me. He sent me here. I'm sorry to disturb, mistress."

She frowned at her reflection, but didn't bother to stand. "Let yourself in."

Chapter Four
Sandals for the Mistress

LAINIOUS CAME INTO the room and shut the door behind him. His eyes sought hers. When they stared at each other, Althyn realized the control she already had over this man. He carried a burlap sack with him, and his chest rose and fell with each nervous breath. Taller than her, he had to duck beneath the doorway. "You have need of sandals?" he asked in a low voice.

She tied off the final braid, appraising his chest. "Yes. My uncle said you can make them for me."

Lainious nodded. He set his bag on the planked floor, opened it, and rifled through for what he needed. While he bent over, she noticed the thin scars across his back. She hadn't seen them before on the island. They caught the light, white lines lashed there some time ago.

"Are you a slave?" she asked, curious. He didn't seem as wont to gawk at her as the others. His demure nature reminded her of how she had acted before her mother's death.

Lainious shot her a quick glance. "Yes." He drew out a square of leather and metal tools. "I will need to measure your feet."

She walked to him and stood there, studying his craft. "Do it then."

Lainious's fingers shook as he reached for her left foot. He touched her toes, one by one and shook his head. "Do you want me to wash them?"

She frowned. Indeed her feet were filthy, sullied by traipsing about in the wilds. "Yes." She stepped away, the light trace of his fingertips vanishing. Sitting upon the side of her mother's bed, she waited for the man to fetch a bucket. He bowed before her and washed each foot with a warm, wet rag. His fingers delved into the arches of her feet. She sighed, but said nothing. With a slip of dry fabric, he wiped away the water. Glancing up with ocean blue eyes, he sought approval with his forced smile.

"How did you come to be on my father's ship?"

Lainious slid the square of hard leather beneath her feet, tracing them with a bit of coal. "Your father stole me from the Assantra of Daius. He took many things from her, jewels, relics..."

Althyn raised a brow. "Really?" She wriggled her toes when he pulled the leather out and began to snip it with his shears. "How long ago was this?"

"I have lost count of the moons since then."

"And what did you do for this...Assantra?"

His blue eyes showed for a moment, then he glanced back to his work, haunted as the sea that spoke to her. "I cooked and cared for her children."

"There are no children here," Althyn muttered. "I suppose you cook."

"And clean the deck. I knot the nets when we're at sea for too long. I'm useful."

"I have no need for men that aren't." She lay back on her bed and stared at the silks quivering with each gentle toss the ship made. "They will mutiny against me."

"Yes, mistress. There is talk of it already." A bit of leather dropped to the floor with a soft plunk. The snips grated.

"And what of you, Lainious?" She closed her eyes and listened to his slow breathing, the rhythmic tone of his shears and, nearly hidden but always there, the songs of the waves calling her name. "Will you stand against me?"

Another scrap of leather fell. "I will go with the one that claims me, as I always have. I belonged to your father and now, I belong to you."

She smiled. "That's right. You're mine. Your loyalty will be rewarded." She lifted one foot and stretched to touch his shoulder with her toes. The snipping halted. He held his breath. "Do you think I'm beautiful?"

Waves roiled and churned outside. A wind picked up, screeching somewhere in the distance. Althyn felt connected to the world, to the water that surrounded her vessel, but she felt nothing for this slave before her. She wanted to test him, to see what he might do. He was nice to look upon, but he was no challenge, not a man to be battled, for he had been broken long ago.

"The Assantra kept many women in her palace, some from all over the lands. They were beautiful, mistress, but..."

She lifted her head to peer down at him. Their gazes locked. She saw the wonder in his blue eyes, the lost look of a man mesmerized. "Say it."

"None like you."

As he stared at her, his mouth slightly ajar, Althyn realized something about herself. Beauty was one thing, but her mermish blood changed what men saw, made her appealing in a way she couldn't fathom. Suddenly her father's words, when she'd found him in the jungle standing over her mother's remains, made sense. She sat up and pushed a braid from her shoulder. "You would do anything for me, wouldn't you?"

He licked his lower lip with the tip of his pink tongue, his eyes fixed. "Anything you ask."

She stood and walked around her slave. She traced his bare shoulder with her forefinger, marveling at this newfound gift. Certainly, she hadn't held this strength over her father, but maybe their shared blood negated its power. Her hand slipped up Lainious's neck and across his tense cheek. She furled her fingers in his thick curls and hummed.

He closed his eyes and leaned his head back in ecstasy. "Your voice," he said, breathless. His shears fell from his grip and onto the wood.

Lured to find out more, she knelt before him and cupped his face with both hands. She sang a light melody her mother had taught her as a child, a sweet, lilting lullaby in a tongue she had no name for…until now.

He is handsome, she mused, thinking that his black hair reminded her of her father. He was more muscular though, not as sinewy or lean, and his skin wasn't as dark. With the pads of her thumbs, she traced his lips and leaned closer, somehow caught in the spell she wove as she sang. The man remained helpless, his pupils dancing behind closed lids, his increasingly heavy exhales tickling her fingertips. *What would it be like to kiss him? To force my mouth over his as my father did to my mother?*

She leaned in. Her chest brushed his. He flinched, and she dipped her face so that their lips grazed together. Althyn's words died in her throat. Realizing what danger she might be putting herself in, she sat back and released his cheeks.

"What are you doing to me?" Lainious asked, his eyebrows rising. "It's as if I'm in a dream."

She felt it too, a wisp-like shadow of lavender-gray mist that tried to close in on her mind. Althyn blinked to ward off the effect. She backed away from him and sat before the mirror, realizing the chair had been her father's favorite. "I don't know what you mean," she countered, feeling vulnerable and disliking the panic it caused her. "I'm doing nothing to you. You're imagining things."

She shifted her attention to the wooden chest near the bed, the place she kept her first two weapons, one for her mother and one for her father, trying to put the man out of her thoughts. *Maybe I should kill him now. Kill all of them except Anthis. I can't trust any but my uncle.* Her eyes narrowed. She longed to hold the sword once more, to swing its blade high and finish off some unsuspecting rogue.

"Yes," Lainious whispered, setting back to his task. "Imagining things."

For a moment she pitied him, but her empathy was soon lost. He was a man after all, and the only males in her life thus far left her lacking in security. She didn't want to kiss this one, much less any other. "How long will it be before you finish my sandals?"

"I will have them for you by nightfall, mistress." He took out another piece of leather and began cutting the straps.

"I want beads on them." She reached for the mirror and touched the glass, staring at him in the reflection. "And tooled designs on the edges…flowers. Beautiful things to make me remember my childhood, so that I know I can walk away from it as I've done today and never look back."

"Yes, mistress."

She grew tired as he worked there on the floor, silent save for the clink of a tool or the rubbing of leather. Althyn eventually returned to the bed and curled up beneath the coverlet. It smelled of her mother, sweet and lost. She refused to cry for her, scorning the woman for choosing such a vile mate. *I will not make the same mistake as she. The world is mine to take. I will sample all it has to offer before I lay my soul down for some fool to beat and shred.* Hatred danced in her thoughts as she drifted to sleep.

"MISTRESS?" A WARM palm rested against her hand, rubbing side to side in a gentle fashion.

Althyn opened her eyes and squinted up at Lainious. His face looked worn, darkness creeping under his eyes. She decided his eyes were his shining attribute. Clear and large, they made her want to get lost there, but she did not. She moaned and stretched, relieving herself of his touch. "How long before we reach Truias?" she asked him, smacking her lips together as she woke.

"A day more, mistress. Your sandals are ready. If you would care to try them, I'll make sure they fit and take my leave of you. The others will talk if I stay much longer." He lowered his head.

"Talk of what?" For an instant she wanted to grasp his curly hair and force him to look at her. The urge overwhelmed her, and she found her hand reaching, stopping only when he spoke again.

"A lady should not keep company with men."

Giving in to the urge, she sank her fingers into his thick hair and tugged. He raised his face, his eyes cloudy.

"I am no lady. Make no mistake of that." Energy waved through her body, hot, liquid and burning with passion. Her heart pounded inside her chest. The strangeness of it troubled Althyn. She wondered what was happening to her. All her years she'd been steady in her emotions, but now they roiled and slammed inside her, straining to break free. "If they talk about me in such a way, I'll cut their tongues out."

Lainious's eyebrows furrowed with confusion. "Yes, mistress."

She pulled his head higher, staring at the vein by his throat. His heart pounded too, in time with hers. *Curious.* Her fingers fell away. She shoved the covers back to bare her feet for him. "Lace them up. I will go to the deck now and watch the sea."

Lainious caught his breath. He nodded and changed position to place the sandals on her feet. Lacing them with care, he scarce made a sound. "Are they to your liking?"

She turned her feet this way and that. "They will do." Beads glittered at her. He'd worked toolings of ivy and budding flowers along the laces and the bands that held the sandals to her ankles. "I suppose I will need boots as well. Make me a pair, soft ones."

"Yes, mistress." He turned to leave.

She pushed off the bed, standing behind him. The top of her head just reached his shoulder. She traced a scar across his back. "It was painful, wasn't it?"

He nodded.

"Did my father give you these?" She touched another, and then one more, pressing at the gnarled line of flesh.

"Yes, mistress."

She sighed and bypassed him, walking slow to accustom herself to shoes. So far, she didn't like the feeling, but if this was something they did on the mainland, in the places her uncle spoke of, then she would do it as well.

Chapter Five
Sister's Touch

THE CREWMEMBERS WATCHED her as Althyn took careful steps across the deck, their heavy gazes like flames lapping at dry wood, ready to incinerate their meal. She held her head high, glancing over each surly face, each jagged scar. They were elves, probably from wherever her father came from. He certainly hadn't stayed long enough on her mother's island to call it home. Some had silver hair that drifted in the night breeze. Others had lank, black hair like Anthis and her father. For a moment, she felt uncertain. *There are too many of them. If they band together, they'll overpower me.*

She hurried her pace and stood at the bow of the ship. A great, carved statue of a bare-breasted woman adorned the vessel below her. Salted sea air blew back Althyn's hair and wrestled with her braids. Wisps of her golden tresses swept across her line of vision. Here, as the ship cut its path through the sea, she heard singing far beneath the waves. Her heart picked up its pace. She longed to see one of her kind and leaned across the railing to seek out some glimpse of a mer.

Shadows played beneath the waves. Foam churned on the crests. She saw little in the coming night. Fingers curled around her upper arm, wrenching her backward. She struggled to regain her balance and glared up at the wiry elf that held her, his eyes like two pieces of cut, black glass shadowed beneath an angry brow.

"You would take the slave to your bed before us?" He yanked her toward him. She fell against his chest and stared up at his cruel face.

Behind the cabin, she heard her uncle's voice. "Let her alone, Caith. She is her father's daughter." He cleared his throat. Boot steps trudged and thumped. "And her mother's..."

"Her mother should have been back on Trinere. Who is Arin to take a second wife?" Caith turned Althyn around and shoved her, forcing her toward the cabin.

She tried to pull her arm from his grip, but failed. Her sudden panic shifted to anger. "Arin is dead. Let go of me, or you'll see what my uncle speaks of." She hoped he would heed her warning. *And what did he mean about a second wife*?

"Why should I believe you? Anthis could be lying. I'll find out. Hold you down for a time and see what manner of words sputter from your pretty mouth.' He squeezed hard. Pain etched into her muscle.

Her anger seethed within, causing warmth to burst forth in her chest. All around the ship, the sea grew silent. The wind died. Sails went lax, and Althyn narrowed her eyes. "Try it," she whispered. She stood on the balls of her feet, her sandals straining, and glared into his black eyes.

Caith raised his free hand, balling it into a fist. His upper lip curled in a leering snarl. When he drew his arm back to strike her face, ice crackled along the deck. Crystals of pale cold formed across his arched eyebrows. His hair dripped and then frosted over. A startled cry broke from his lips and died in his throat. The ice didn't halt in its vengeance, encompassing the elf until it held him still and defenseless, his lips tinged with blue.

She pulled free from his grip and spat at his feet. The rest of the crew gathered around them. Some watched her with a new sense in their expressions, the glittery-eyed gape of fear. Others closed in, anxious to avenge their companion.

"A sorceress," one whispered.

"She's trapped him in ice. Impossible!"

"We should send her to the sea, and let the Fates have her. She is not like us..." The crews' shouts of fear and panic slurred the silence in the air. They shuffled about, unsure of what to do next.

Anthis cleared his throat. "Are you all right, my lass?" he asked, skulking ever closer.

She nodded, her eyes stuttering over each crew member. Only three feared her enough to hang near the back of the others. Lainious appeared from the cabin and lingered at the doorway, gripping the jamb with one hand. She stared for a moment at his widened blue eyes.

"I don't need them, Uncle!" she shouted.

"Now, lass, you do. Who will hoist the sails and steer? Who will clean the decks and cast nets when we're at sea for days at a time? We need a crew to keep the ship on course and in good order." He raised his hands at the others. "All of you know me. You knew my brother. I ask, would you defy him if he stood in his daughter's place? It is with good reason that she captains Arin's ship."

"We should avenge his death!" A gnarled elf grabbed up a fistful of Althyn's hair. He pierced her with his amber gaze and licked his lips feverishly. "Slit your throat. Toss you to the sharks, we will."

"Try it." She stepped close to him rather than retreat. Her chest poked into his, and she pressed her lips into a tight line.

Unfaltering, he strode toward the side rail, holding fast to her hair, clearly determined to throw her over. She kept pace with him, unwilling to appear weak. One hand curled into his shirt. She felt the sea's call and also, a new sensation. The very water in the air pooled near, waiting to do her bidding, much as it had done to the frozen elf.

"Shame to waste such a fair beauty," her attacker muttered.

For an instant, she saw the flash of lust in his eyes. She drew on it naturally now, beginning to master the trick. She forced a slow smile, her lips parting. "Kiss me goodbye then. See if I taste as sweet as you imagine."

His angry eyes turned glassy. His snarl of a mouth lowered.

"That's right," she urged. As it had deep in the sea, her body responded to her will. Her short fingernails, always worn down from chores on the island, lengthened. They grew swiftly, cutting past his shirt, past skin and sinking between the gaps of his ribs. His mouth opened to gasp or perhaps to cry out in pain, but she leaned forward and pressed her mouth over his lips. Her skin crawled. He tasted bad, like strong wine and sour cheese.

In a single, gruff motion, she dragged her newfound talons up and shoved the man over the ship's side. His body fell, and he didn't scream until he hit the water. Her hand slicked with warm blood, she craned to watch his death. Behind her, she half-heard the crew's softer mutterings and her uncle's continued arguments to sway them to favor her.

Concentrating, she decided she wanted the drowning man to dip below the waves. Around his bobbing head, water pinked and clouded. She frowned and whispered to the sea. "Take him. A gift to sate your desire for me." Waves rose high and thundered over her attacker. *Is there no end to what I can do?*

Althyn held her malformed hand before her face. It was not a mermish transformation. She wriggled her scaled fingers, the talons clicking together, black beneath the slur of blood. "Sister?" she questioned, recognizing their shape.

Boots trod behind her. A familiar, sweaty palm closed over her shoulder and neck. "Lass. I think your mother was right. You remember what she said. Perhaps you should go on to the waves of Yneria's birth."

Her talons retracted. Skin twisted and curled. Bits of flesh fell away and dropped down to the hungry water. She made sure her hand appeared normal before she spun to confront her uncle. The only trace of wrongdoing, other than the missing crewmember, was the glistening blood staining her pale fingers. "I know what she said. I know her end. After this day, we will not speak of my parents or what they wanted for me again. Do you understand me, Uncle?" She stared him down, a newly made predator asserting her dominance.

He backed away, a silent nod affirming his assent. His hand dropped to his side.

Althyn smirked. "Good." She peered around her uncle's side at the remaining crew. Silent as she counted, her gaze darted from elf to elf. There were thirteen remaining, which included Lainious and Anthis. "I wish to watch the sea now!" She paced before the elf who had first confronted her. The crew stood to the sides of her, watching. The sails had yet to catch a breeze. Stagnant in the water by her will alone, the vessel too, waited.

Anthis murmured to her. "We need them."

"No!" she spat. "We do *not!* Those who wish to meet the same end as these last two, come for me now. If you want to live, then toss this one over the side." She gestured to the ice-encrusted elf. "If you leave him here, the dawn will melt him and he'll start to stink." She strode to the bow without waiting for their response.

Every nerve in her body felt afire. Each breath she took in tasted of the sea and the many scents around her. She knew the pleasure of freedom and sank into the dangerous hold of power. It filled her.

Boot steps clunked against the deck. Voices channeled through the unmoving air, muttering about a sorceress, a vile demoness that had escaped the depths of the underworld to take over their ship. No matter how they talked behind her back, they obeyed. The crash of the elf's body into the sea caused Althyn to smile.

She hummed a livelier tune under her breath, one she used to dance to in the mornings after her mother had done the washing. Her bare feet would leave trails in the smooth sand by the shore and her mother's face held such peace, as if she saw heaven when she looked upon her daughter.

Sorrow stung her mind, but she pushed it back. Althyn's voice wavered, and then just as suddenly, came out stronger, ghostly in its hypnotic beauty. The wind obeyed and gathered against the sails. The waves shifted, parting to lure the ship forward. She sang with vigor, pride, and arrogance curling through her heart. She knew what she kept telling her uncle was true. *I don't need them, not even one.*

Anthis shouted at the crew, his hoarse voice hardly audible beneath Althyn's song. They went about their duties, most vanishing from the bow to lurk in the shadows or otherwise remain out of sight of their new mistress. She finished her song and turned to inspect the emptiness. Lainious bowed his head from his vantage by the cabin door. She nodded, acknowledging his quiet loyalty.

Pleased, Althyn leaned over the statue of the woman at the bow and began a new song. She wanted to sing long into the night, perhaps until dawn. The sun set at last and the stars came into being across the horizon before her. She breathed in the cooling air that bit past her dress. Her stomach grumbled, reminding her she needed to eat.

She listened to the air and the sea melding as one in their simple music. Resigning to her hunger, she left the ship's head to find the one servant who attended her needs. She thought of the flag she planned to raise, a tribute to her fallen gryphon, a majestic banner of blue with the creature's image emblazoned in white. "Lainious," she called into the darkness. He stood in the hall near her door, the lack of light hiding his expression.

"Yes, mistress?"

"I have another task for you to complete."

Chapter Six
The Port of Truias

AFTER LAINIOUS HAD gathered her a heaping plate of cheese, bread, and fruit, Althyn draped herself across the bed to nibble and stare at her servant. He sat cross-legged on the floor, a length of fabric in his lap and a needle ready for threading. His attention caught on her for a tense moment before he set to work. She sipped at a goblet of wine and cleared her throat. "The Assantra was a queen of sorts, correct?"

He poked at the fabric, drawing a thin line of white string high, only to dip back and poke the needle in a second time. Without looking up, Lainious replied, "More like a guardian of relics. I believe that's why your father killed her. Simply to steal the treasures of the sect."

She leaned forward."Sect?"

"The Assantra was a high leader in the Othian Church. They keep a number of women there, cloistered away. Some are allowed to bear children, but only with approved mates devout to the faith."

She crinkled her nose at him. "Sounds boring. Tell me who rules Truias. Where are all the relics and riches there?"

Lainious sewed, his face emotionless. He sighed before he spoke. "Truias is a port town. Mostly fishers and merchants line the docks. There's not a great deal of wealth, but if a man is said to rule it or to hold any power over its people, that man would be Lord Jabir Salak. I cannot say if he keeps relics, but he has an estate anyone can see from the piers."

Althyn sliced an apple with a small knife. She ate the precisely cut pieces in delicate bites, thinking. On the one hand, she loathed to follow in her father's footsteps; on the other, the idea of thieving valued relics from a pompous politician or lord intrigued her. She sipped at the wine. "Tell me more about this lord."

"My mistress, I know only a little of the hearsay that drifts to a servant when we make port. Your father never let me wander far or speak much. Besides, I am no storyweaver."

She listened to the fabric and thread's little song. Lainious remained devout in his work. She wondered if he knew what it felt like to be free, if he'd always been a slave. She would have to ask him about his past later, but for now, he held little interest for her, other than as a source of information about the outside world. "Storyweaver? What is that?"

"A teller of tales, a person that spins stories for entertainment." He paused, his eyes sparkling as he regarded her. "Oh, I remember the Assantra's storyweaver. She would speak to the children before bed. She told them glorious adventures, stories of sea monsters and magic, of far-off kingdoms where mystical treasures waited to be found."

"Then I shall have a storyweaver," she whispered, entranced by the idea. Althyn finished her meal and set the plate on the floor near her servant. She tugged at the bedcovers and climbed beneath them. "Keep the door barred," she told him. "I'm going to sleep."

"Yes, mistress." She lay on her side listening to his sewing and the churn of the waves outside. At last, Althyn drifted into her dreams. In the first, she swam in the sea, weightless and empty of heart. She searched for someone, but who, she didn't know, only that she must find—him. The dream faded, and she found herself on the island by the ruins of her mother's home. No one greeted her there. The place remained as empty and silent as ever.

A familiar voice called to her. "Whore. Let me out of here."

She sneered in her dream, knowing full well that her father lingered between the world of the living and the dead. "You come to me in my dreams now? You never bothered to pay any mind to me before."

"Break the axe," he ordered.

She chuckled at him. "You have no power over me. I'll carry that axe to the day I die and before then, pass it along to some *relic guardian* to protect. There you will suffer and know the loneliness my mother bore every time you went away."

She felt a pang of fear, much like the tension in her body just before he'd strike her. Her dream was interrupted by a hand tracing hers, back and forth.

"Mistress, it is done."

She opened her eyes. Lainious stood by the bed, his hand still on hers, his fingers cold. He took a step backward and held the flag before his body for inspection.

Half-awake, she blinked at the image, a proud gryphon, its white wings spread wide, its beak sharp and its pale, cat-like body arced in a defensive pose. Tears welled in her eyes. She thought of the day she found her sister on the crags, how the little creature had purred when she hoisted the gryphon up in her arms.

"Well done," she said. "Go and fly my colors." She settled further into the pillows and raised her arms to stretch. "How much longer until we reach the pier?"

Lainious smiled. "My mistress, we are almost there. The sun came not long ago."

She merely nodded and rolled onto her side. "Wake me when we reach the dock." Althyn tugged the coverlet over her head, listening to him unbar the door and leave. She tried to rest a little more, but soon the sounds of seagulls irritated her. The crew's heavy footfalls above deck only added to her darkening mood.

The door to her room creaked. "My lass," her uncle cooed. "We have reached Truias. Come on board and see the mainland." The feather-stuffed mattress sank under his weight when he sat beside her and tugged at her hiding place. "Did you not sleep enough?"

She opened one eye, squinting up at him. He looked weary, his nasty hair stringier than usual. "I had nightmares."

Concern twisted his expression, fouling it more so. "We'll go to the bathhouse. They have heated water there. You can have your hair done up...buy a new dress, one that suits you. You'll like Truias."

Her other eye opened. "Bathhouse?"

"Yes, lass." He tugged the coverlet down.

She sat up slowly, holding her forehead. "All right. Let me change."

"Be sure to wear a veil over your face." Anthis patted her knee, offering an encouraging smile.

"Why should I cover my face?" His request made her curious. "I have a fair face. I've seen myself in the looking glass." She waved a hand at the mirror. "There is nothing to hide."

"A woman of importance does not allow those lower born than her to see her face." Anthis stood, readying to leave.

"Oh." She shimmied off the bed and stood beside the chest of her mother's clothes. "Go on then," she ordered, waving him out. "Give me privacy."

TOGETHER UNCLE AND niece emerged in the bright sunlight of dawn. The sails snapped in the wind. Gulls dipped low, braving the dives to seek out scraps on the ship's deck. Althyn stared at the mainland, an endless line crossing the horizon they faced. She tried to count the docks, but failed. "There are so many." She had trouble comprehending the vastness of civilization, never having encountered it before.

Anthis pointed at a building that stood far behind the strip of shops and smoking chimneys. Althyn followed his direction and stared at the stone manor atop a hill, an enormous estate with gold flags whipping in the wind. "That is where the lord resides. He collects taxes from the entire city and another beyond the hills. These people," he waved his hand across the docks, "they fish and peddle their wares day in, day out. Some imports come from the east, a few ships from the south. I will show you the wonders you've always asked me about."

Althyn knew her uncle's pride. His knowledge gave him weight over her, but she swore it would not always be so. She kept her gaze on the manor. *If this lord collects tithes from so many people, he must be rich beyond measure. He must have treasures and relics.* Her ship edged close to an empty dock. A silver-haired elf tossed down the anchor. Another jumped over the side to catch the rope. Soon the crew all gathered to make their way down the plank to dry land, shooting backward glances her way.

Althyn and Anthis ventured to the railing. She looked over her shoulder for her servant, unwilling to go far without him. Lainious comforted her in a way. Although she didn't want to depend on him, his quiet demeanor and fast loyalty eased her. He stood near the cabin, his hands full of nets and the dark circles beneath his eyes attesting to a night lacking in sleep. "Are you coming?" she called to him.

"There's mending to be done, mistress." He held up the nets to prove his words.

"No. There will be time to mend them later. I want you with me." She motioned him over and waited to descend until he walked just behind her. Althyn supposed it was all he knew, the way he'd been taught, to follow at a master's heels. Her forearm remained laced in the crook of her uncle's arm. They crossed the wooden planks to the gravel road.

The scents of roasting fish, fresh fish, and even the rancid odor of fish that had sat in the sun too long assaulted her. Each booth they passed indeed held treasures, swatches of bright fabric, painted boxes, carvings, so many wonderful things she longed to stop and touch or inspect closer. Anthis kept her moving along. She tugged at his arm. "I want to see the wares."

"Bath first," he explained.

Ahead, she glimpsed members of the crew disappearing into an arched doorway. At either side, women lifted their skirts, leering and taunting more to come inside. "What is that, Uncle?" She craned her neck to see inside when they stopped at the entry. Althyn stared at one woman's bared knees.

"It's no place for a lady such as yourself." Anthis pulled at her arm, but she remained, curious and in need of an explanation. "Althyn, this is a brothel."

She slipped her arm from his grasp. "I want to see the inside." She took a step toward the woman in red and touched her dress, admiring the fine fabric.

The woman smiled and giggled. "You are welcome to join us," she offered with a batting of her painted lashes.

Ignoring her, Althyn nodded at her uncle. "These ladies are here." She pointed inside to the stage of dancers and tables stationed about the show. "Look there, Uncle, I see others."

Anthis took her hand and led her away. "I'll explain it to you over our meal. Come, child. This is no place for you."

Behind her, Lainious chuckled. She glanced at him and frowned. "Is there not a brothel for ladies?"

Lainious shook his head, humor dancing in his blue eyes.

"Ah just there," Anthis stated, pointing a grime-stained finger at a white-washed building. "A hot bath and a hot drink. Heaven awaits, my lass." He hurried his pace and she followed, wishing more than ever to go exploring through the merchant's wares to see just what he was hiding from her in that brothel.

Chapter Seven
Bathing

THEY WEAVED THEIR way through the muddle of people and entered an inn. The main room bustled with patrons drinking and eating or otherwise entertaining themselves with dance. Althyn wanted to stop and watch them turning circles about. She wanted to sit and listen to the lively music and to breathe in the woody taste of pipe smoke. Anthis ushered her into another room, though. He explained their needs to a large woman whose breasts looked about ready to pop over the bodice of her green dress.

"This way," the matron said. Her round face pinched while she gave Althyn an appraising glance. "The women bathe apart from the men here." She motioned for them to follow.

A sweet scent permeated the air of the small room they entered. Perfumes and colored soaps lined the shelves. A tub molded of metal centered the room, steam drifting from the water it held. Althyn lifted a jar of colored salts and turned it this way and that, thinking the contents looked like gemstones.

"This room is for the lady," the attendant explained. "I'll take you two to the men's side."

Althyn turned, surprised to be left alone so suddenly. A prickle of panic made her tense. "Uncle, be sure Lainious is bathed as well." She crinkled her nose in her servant's direction, further showing her meaning.

"Of course," Anthis replied, his dark eyebrows bunching together.

When they'd taken their leave, she discarded her veil, stripped, and sank into a tubful of heated water. Mist rose about the air in snaking wisps. Tense muscles relaxed. She closed her eyes. The sweet perfume in the bathwater reminded her of wildflowers back home. Just as she was about to drift to sleep, someone shouted in the hall outside her room.

The man's voice, deep and resonant, jarred her awake. She sat up, eyes narrowing in angst. Anger came so rushed into her moods now. She frowned at the door and then, it burst open.

"Where are you hiding him? He owes taxes!" The man dragged the heavy chested attendant into the chamber. He wore thick armor, dull and stained from use. Chainmail clinked in time with his thudding footfalls. Bloodstains swiped across his high cheekbone on the left side of his face. His black-bearded jaw was square, set in a hateful expression that reminded Althyn of her father. Her heart pounded.

The attendant blubbered. She'd been hit already, her right eye swelling.

"Get out," Althyn whispered. She gripped the sides of the tub, alarmed that she had no weapon nearby, not that she thought it would have much effect on this intruder.

The man spied her as if only noticing the room held an occupant. He froze. His grim expression faltered. The knob in his throat bobbled when he swallowed. Releasing the woman, he took a step toward Althyn, his dark eyes widening. "You..." His thick eyebrows rose and fell, confusion changing to awe.

Althyn stood. Water dripped from her bare skin. She felt no shame, no need to hide herself from him. Her temper flared, twisting with a euphoric drive to control him. "Come here," she ordered him, holding out one hand. Bits of his thoughts drifted in her mind to mingle with her anger.

Beautiful...woman...can't be...real.

He wiped at his temple and lurched forth, clumsy, as if unable to stop himself.

The room buzzed with the same euphoric sensation Althyn felt on board the ship when she'd been alone with Lainious. Her heart thrummed in her ears. Her body, already hot from the water, felt afire. She took stock of the myriad weapons dangling from the man's thick belt; two daggers, a sword, a mace of sorts and a leather pouch, which intrigued her curiosity. When his fingers came into hers, she felt thick skinned calluses there from holding the handle of a blade.

She squeezed his hand. "What is your name?"

He chewed the side of his cheek before answering. "Tolston. I'm Lord Salak's high guard."

"Ah." She stepped out of the bath and let go of his fingers. He stood much taller than her, so she craned her neck to stare up into his face.

His gaze burned over her nudity. He licked his lips in wanton expectation. Regaining a hold over a portion of his mind, for the slips of his thoughts ceased, he reached up and snared a handful of her wet hair. "What are you?" He leaned down, studying her eyes, his pupils flicking side to side, judging, trying to understand. "I've never seen a woman like you." His other hand rose. Dropping her hair, he pushed it away from her face and examined her ears. "Ha, elf mix. Still...there is something I cannot place..."

"Tolston!" Another armed man filled the doorway, drawing Althyn's attention, further breaking the mysterious hold she had on the first. This one did not carry as much muscle-bound weight. He strode into the room, casting a swift glance at the cowering attendant. "Bartholomew was in the kitchens. I found him." He held up a woven pouch. When he shook it, coins jingled.

"Ha! Paid then." Tolston turned back to Althyn, grasped her chin between his thumb and forefinger and lifted her face. "I'm sorry to disturb your bath, lady." He held her chin in place and lowered his mouth to hers. He pressed a hard kiss there. Tolston smelled like sweat and leather oil. He tasted of ale, the same flavor permeating the air where the people danced when she first came to this place. His beard grated across her skin, the brash advance shocking her. Pulling away, he murmured, "Maybe I'll see you again." Turning on his heel, he left her standing there in a puddle of bathwater.

The second man shook his head, his ardent gaze curiously trained on her face. He dared not look lower, as the first one had, and his words revealed a different agenda, much more noble than the first man's. "Forgive him," he muttered with discomfort. "My brother is arrogant."

"Mathea, come, get up and offer this lady a wrap." He waved a hand at the woman in the corner. Released to take up her duties, she obeyed and scurried to do his bidding.

Once the dry fabric draped around her body, the second man offered a half-smile to Althyn. "I'm Doran, one of Lord Salak's high guards." He didn't hold out a hand or move to get closer. "Sometimes the merchants don't pay on time and we…have to…"

Althyn cleared her throat and turned her back on him. He was too kind, too soft and well-mannered. The scorching heat she felt when the first man touched her had yet to fade. "Leave," she ordered, holding up a hand. "Tell your brother he will pay for disturbing me."

"*What* did you say?" He sounded aghast at her words.

"Your brother will pay. Tell him I said so." She crossed the room and fingered a basket laden with molded soaps. Glancing over her shoulder, she weighed the guard a second time to be sure she hadn't misjudged his character. His expression said it all. He was shocked by her nature and even embarrassed that his brother had done what he did. "And you. Get out!" she shouted. Curling her fingers around a bar of soap, she raised it and hurled it at the guard's face.

It hit his cheek, and he backed into the hall, holding a hand to the injury. "I-I'm sorry," he stammered. He had the same eyes as his brother, darkly intense, only less scrutinizing.

"You tell him!"

The guard backed away, disappearing into the hall and the rooms beyond.

"Where's my uncle?" Althyn snapped at the attendant. "What sick place is this he's brought me to?"

The woman shook her head. "Gone, Lady. He tried to escape the back way, but Tolston caught him and tied him with the other criminals. Said they been lookin' for him for months."

"What!" Althyn could hardly believe what the woman had said. She turned on the shelves and clenched a fist, her eyes narrowing. She swiped her arm and sent all the bottles and baskets careening to the floor.

The attendant gasped and retreated to the corner.

"Where is my servant?" Althyn pulled on her dress before she started for the open doorway, rage surging inside her mind and body, ready to burst.

"Th-they took him, too. Said he was property of the Othian Church. He was marked." Her wide brown eyes blinked once. "Marked with an Assantra's sign."

"No! He's mine. They can't take Lainious. He belongs to me!" Forgetting her veil, she marched out of the chamber, down the hall, and stomped through the main room, which now was near empty. Outside the building, a line of guards waited. Ahead of them, Tolston and Doran argued. Althyn didn't care about them. She crossed the guards, her feet bare and burning from the rough gravel road.

"Mistress!" Lainious' low voice drew her attention to a cart of prisoners. He held up his tied wrists and shook his head.

"Get down here!" she raged. "They can't take you."

"Go back to the ship," he told her. "Wait for the crew. They'll know what to do for your uncle."

"I said get down here!" she aimed a rigid finger at the ground. "Now!"

"Mistress, please," Lainious murmured. "Do not draw attention to yourself and for your sake, say nothing of your uncle, of your surname. They'll hang you beside Anthis if they find out."

A string of wet hair fell across her forehead. She swiped it back and set her gaze on the high guards. "No." Stomping toward them, she ignored her servant's pleas to be silent, to hide on the ship and wait for someone else to help her.

"You!" she screeched, aiming her angry finger at Tolston. "Give me back my servant! You have no right to take what's mine!"

Tolston laughed when she approached, lines crinkling at the sides of his eyes. "I hadn't expected to see you again so soon, pretty one." He snatched up her hand and tugged her against his armored chest. "Surely there's been some mistake, some oversight. Lord Salak's laws are clear. Show me this servant of yours."

The closeness of him overwhelmed her with more of his thoughts, lascivious wanderings and hints of what he'd like to do to her in a chamber alone. She shirked off his hold.

"That one!" she shouted, singling Lainious out. "The one with the black hair. He belongs to me."

Tolston squinted at the prisoners. He strode ahead of Althyn and tapped the side of the cart. "I don't think so, pretty one." He snagged a hold of Lainious's pants, tugging him closer. "This one's marked." Tolston tugged down Lainious's clothing a bit, revealing a dark insignia just below his navel. "You see that?"

Althyn shook her head. "What does it matter who owned him before? He's mine now. You get him down from there, out of that filth!"

"Look, lady. Anything with the mark of the Othians is returned to the Othians. Salak doesn't want a curse on crops or fishing. The priestess' magic is as strong as ever. These days lords can't afford to— "

"No!" She stepped forward and tried to grab Lainious' leg. At the same moment, Tolston shoved the servant backwards. Lainious fell amongst the hay in the cart. The high guard whistled through his teeth, signaling the driver, and the cart lurched forth.

He clutched her upper arm and squeezed tight. "I don't know what kind of game you're playing with me. That man belongs to the church, not some half-breed. I don't care how pretty you are. He's going back where he belongs."

"I'll get you for this," she hissed.

He laughed once more, his dark eyes alight with mischief. "Careful, pretty one. I may just get *you*. Take you back to the tower and show you who is master."

She spit in his face.

He wiped it away with his free hand and shook his head. "You need your spirit broken." Leaning down, he whispered in her ear, his breath warm. "Want me to break it for you?"

His closeness antagonized her. Rage burst in her chest, and she saw only white-hot fury, not the face that leered at her. Althyn shook free of Tolston's grip. Her fingernails burned to elongate, to shift into claws. She wanted to scratch out his eyes first and then—

"Leave the woman. You've bothered her enough for one day!" Doran came between them, ushering Althyn to the walkway. "I'm sorry a second time. For your trouble." He pressed a pouch of coins into her palm and started away.

Alone and irritated, she stood there and watched the procession pass down the main road. She wanted to find Anthis, to get her servant back, and more than anything she wanted to put that arrogant high guard in his place.

Chapter Eight
Abandoned and Alone

RAIN DRIZZLED ON the port town as Althyn sauntered along the docks toward her ship. The weather reflected her mood, gray and angry with no other outlet but to spit on everything around her. She'd gone back for her sandals. Now they were wet, squeaking where the leather touched the bottoms of her feet. She stomped up the plank to the ship's deck and glanced around. It didn't look like anyone had returned, but they might be below deck, avoiding the weather, she reasoned. The gryphon flag flapped in the wind, soggy and grim.

She hurried through the cabin door and heard no one inside. Checking each door, each room she found empty, the chests devoid of personal effects and not much left of any interest. Her crew had mutinied in the most silent of ways, not that she expected them to stay. They had, however, left her room untouched. She wondered if it was superstition. She sat at the foot of the bed and stared at her mother's chest. "I should take the axe and chop off his head," she whispered, thinking of the man who had stolen Anthis and Lainious. "Cut him to pieces and then the other one, too."

But death wasn't exactly what she wanted for Tolston. Althyn didn't understand her conflicting emotions. She hated his impetuous nature, the way he grabbed her and held her still, and yet she craved his attention if only to have it. Groaning, she kicked off her sandals and moved to sit before the mirror. Even sodden, with her hair mussed and stringy, she looked beautiful. She leaned forward to study the sea green color of her eyes.

"*Break the axe.*"

"Be silent," she told the voice. "I've no wish to hear you." She shivered and began to unlace her dress bindings. "I have more important things to tend to than spirits."

Outside, the wind picked up its pace, rocking the ship and causing wood to creak. Althyn stripped and paced the room naked, trying to decide her next move. For once, she was entirely alone. She thought of cutting the ropes that held the vessel to the dock and taking her chances at sea. "Maybe I should leave Anthis to fend for himself." She tapped her chin and twisted her mouth. "Not that he ever did anything on his own. He won't escape. They'll keep him in a dungeon or kill him or whatever it is they do."

Her father's voice echoed with chilling laughter in the room—or her mind—she couldn't be sure. Althyn decided to confront her rival now. She opened the chest at the foot of the bed and chose a finer gown, one beaded and embroidered. Remembering the day Anthis gifted it to her mother, she smiled. It was a brief, but happy memory. She slipped the gown over her head and laced the sides, then brushed out her hair and braided it, tying the end with a leather scrap Lainious had left behind.

She uncovered the axe and stared at the weapon, wondering how she could hide it and gain entrance into the Lord's manor. Its bulk would be difficult to disguise. She placed her hands on its marred handle and lifted the weapon. A rush of hatred filled her, anger unbidden and fury that pulsed and filled her thoughts. With a shocked cry, she dropped it. As fast as the rage had filled her, it dissipated.

She pushed the vile axe to one side and reached lower. The long sword called to her in a sweet way, voiceless and without any summons she could explain. It reached into her mind and found purchase there. Althyn held up the sheathed blade and smiled. "Yes. This was meant to be mine." It felt near weightless as it had before. She clutched it to her chest and held it for a time. Last, she dug to the bottom of the piles of clothing, avoiding the axe and seeking a small pouch of coins her mother kept for the fanciful engravings across their round surfaces. With that and the coins Doran had given her, she felt confident that she could do what was necessary.

THE GUARD AT the gate stared at her face. He seemed unable to look away. Althyn smirked. He was a young man with barely a few bristles of stubble on his upper lip. His clear blue eyes blinked and focused, registering that same dumbstruck look she now recognized as a byproduct of whatever mer change affected her. As she passed the guard, she wondered if the magic would fade in time. *Why couldn't my mother do this to my father?* But then, she'd never seen her mother do it to anyone. Even Anthis doted on her of his own will without the same look in his eyes as this man.

"Tolston," she repeated for the fifth time. "I have business with High Guard Tolston. He has something that belongs to me." Standing closer to him didn't help the guard's ability to understand. He slurred his words when he spoke.

"Highgar...Tol..."

She touched his face, slipping her fingers beneath the side guard of his helm. His hair was soft and warm. "Take me to Tolston." Her patience wore thin, and she tried not to glare.

"Of course," he answered. He took her arm and led the way through the gates, blubbering excuses to his fellows about Tolston and the lady collecting her property. The man, who couldn't speak only moments before, found his words and filled the silence non-stop, further irritating Althyn's already dark mood.

Ignoring him, she paid attention to the layout of the grounds surrounding the manor. Sheep grazed in the distance, gated and watched by two young boys. Green grass spread as far as she could see, all the way to the forest. An orchard lined the eastern side of the estate. She entered another set of gates and kept pace with her guide beneath a long archway. Glancing at the brick ceiling, she noticed slits cut out and wondered at their purpose.

"...in the hall for meals at this time of day. And then they'll be dancing. You dance, don't you?" Her escort stopped and smiled at her.

"Dance?" She shook her head, losing patience. "Tolston, you take me to him now." The leather sheath strapped down the back of her dress and hidden by her cloak, itched her skin.

"I'm so sorry; I didn't ask your name...' He grasped her fingers, leaning so close she smelled the sweat on his skin, the mild odor of tallow soap and horse hide.

"Althyn." She frowned and stepped away from him, disturbed by his closeness.

"And how does he know you?"

Her anger and impatience affected her hold on his mind. Clarity glistened in his pupils, dancing through the daze. A dimple appeared between his eyebrows while he awaited her answer.

"He stole my servant." She pushed a fallen wisp of her hair behind one ear. Across the courtyard, well-dressed people milled. Laughter filtered from behind closed doors. The rain had settled not long after she left the ship, and moisture hung heavy in the cooling evening air. Even so far from it, she could smell the taste of the sea. "I want my property back."

Faltering, the guard opened his mouth, closed it, and opened it once more. "Perhaps I should take you to the courts. It's there you must go to report stolen property." His gaze lowered to her chest and fixed there. "And Lady, I must warn you not to press Tolston. He is known for his temper, for his..."

Clearing her throat, she glanced over the guard's shoulder at vines clinging to the stone wall and trellises. Purple flowers glistened with raindrops. Somewhere nearby she heard the sound of rushing water. She left the guard's side, seeking the tranquil music that lured her. A fountain carved of pale marble and gilded at the edges stood beneath another archway. Althyn traced the water's surface, her mind turning with an eerie pain.

"Lady Althyn!" The guard rushed after her. She shook her head, hearing voices far from where she stood, but insistent nevertheless. They sang in unison and though she couldn't understand their pleas, the urge to find them, to join them, made her anxious to leave the manor and abandon her plan to find Lainious and her uncle. She grasped her forehead, wincing.

"Are you ill, Lady?"

Her eyes slipped shut and she heard only the mersong pulsing through the air. The attentive guard hauled her up though she couldn't open her eyes or focus on speaking any intelligible words.

Her body swayed. Someone carried her through halls and past lit torches. Minstrels played a garbled tune nearby, but it didn't match the wonder of the voices carried to her on the breeze. Nothing could match the musical beauty, the fascination she held for their call. "I have to go back..." she whispered.

Doors opened and shut. Men's voices danced and mingled. Amidst her trance-like confusion, she realized the man she sought had surfaced. His deep voice echoed around her. "Put the lady in my room." His now familiar laughter grated on her nerves. "Three times in one day. It's a sign."

A final door slapped shut. Wood rubbed on wood.

She breathed out, and the mersong vanished.

"Well, look at you. Not so furious as this morning." Rough fingers ran along her cheek and neck. "Wake up, pretty one."

She cracked her eyes open and Tolston's squared visage jarred her into reality. Heat built in her chest. She struggled to draw steady breaths, but each came filled with the musky man scent of him. He sat only a hand's length from her, his fingers teasing the lip of her dress above her cleavage.

"Couldn't stay away from me?" He bent over and kissed her lips hard. His fingers tugged at her bodice.

The haze around them thickened, and Althyn gave in to her magic. She grasped clumsily for his face and found his hair, curling her fingers into the thick locks. Arching her back, anxious to taste more of him, to *possess* him, she returned his kiss. Her unexpected passion fueled him on.

A knock sounded on the door.

"Tolston," A feminine voice called. "It's me, Elspeth."

"Go away!" he shouted and went back to his conquest of Althyn's mouth. His breathing rasped. He attacked her neck, sliding his hot tongue across her skin, awakening her body as never before.

"Who is that?" Althyn asked, breathless. "Who's at the door?"

"My mistress." He nipped at her neck, his beard scraping her tender skin. "One of them."

"Mistress?" She pushed at his broad shoulders. He wore soft fabric, a pouf-sleeved tunic with intricate stitchwork along the open neck that felt like flower petals under her fingers.

Tolston hovered over her for a moment and flashed a decadent grin. "Guess I'll add you to the list." He tugged at her bodice and threads snapped.

Althyn let her hand fall on the mattress. Glancing to her right, she found a wall of bookshelves. To her left, another wall that held a different sort of treasure. Blades of all shapes and sizes hung on display, covering the white-washed plaster from ceiling nearly to the floor. She sucked in a surprised breath. "There's so many."

Tolston frowned. He turned toward the wall and then back to her. "What does a woman care for weapons?" He grasped her chin as he'd done that morning and forced her to look at him. "You wouldn't even know how to hold one."

"I would."

Devilish in his provocation, he took up her hand and forced it between their bodies. "I'll teach you how. I'll teach you everything a mistress need know to win my favor." He guided her fingers past his taut stomach to the bulge in his laced up breeches.

Althyn turned her head to the side, eyeing him. She reached up with her free hand, took a handful of his hair and yanked it.

He screeched in fury.

"Master Tolston?" the mistress outside the door called. "Are you all right?"

"Go away I told you!"

Althyn wriggled free and slapped his face. "Bastard," she hissed.

He leered at her and stood, brushing his meaty fingers across his tunic. "You're a feisty little half-breed. I like it better when you look on me with favor. Now your beauty is pinched, your cheeks flushed. I only wish to teach you, to show you how to hold a blade." He smiled halfway, and chuckled once more.

She edged across his ornate bed, a bed much finer than hers, with great carved posts, gilded decorations and linens scented with lavender. Sliding off the opposite side, she backed to the wall of weapons. "You return my servant to me. Now! I want him."

One of his thick eyebrows rose. "You *want* him? I've never seen a lady so attached to a slave. Tell me what he does for you at night, and I'll do it better." He strode around the foot of the bed, effectively cornering her.

"Master Tolston, please?" the lady outside the door screeched. "I need you…to see you…"

"For the last time, woman, go away! I'm busy!" His jaw tightened. He lurched forward and bridged the distance between them. "Pretty one, let me show you how I like to be kissed. I'll shower you with gifts, offer you whatever your heart desires."

He crushed her against the wall. Small blades fell off their hooks and crashed on the stone floor. Althyn struggled to push him away, but his hot mouth tasted of sweet wine and her lips parted so she could explore more of him. She curled her fingers into the softness of his tunic, bunching the fabric in her fists. The headiness returned, a mist of heat and sensation that dulled her rage and made her want him.

Chapter Nine
Sister's Body

WHILE SHE FLOATED in the mesmeric haze of bliss, she became only barely aware that he had destroyed her bodice. The once fine dress dropped from her body and crumpled at her feet. Rough fingers roamed across her skin, exploring every curve, every valley. She closed her eyes and moaned in his mouth.

Tolston pulled away. "What's this?"

His finger caught beneath the fabric binding her sword to her back. He slid his hand up and down the line and chafed the skin between her bared breasts. "No corset?"

She shook her head. "Corset? I don't understand." She had no idea what such a thing was. Her gaze centered on his mouth. She wanted to taste him, to kiss him, to force him onto the bed and tear away his clothes as he'd done to her, but his questing fingers followed the binding across her shoulder. He pursed his delicious lips and then frowned.

"Did you come here to kill me?"

At once, the anger in his tone forced away the spell of passion. She pushed at his chest, longing for freedom from his confinement. He stumbled backward, startled by her sudden strength.

"Yes!" Reaching back, Althyn drew her blade in a clumsy arc. She held it above her head and glared at him. "Give me back my servant and my uncle!" Swiping at the man, she fixed her hatred, hoping to cleave off an arm.

Tolston sidestepped and grasped her wrist, squeezing so hard that she cried out. He slammed a knotted fist against her other arm. Pain lanced there. Her fingers loosened, and the monster of a sword left her hold. It landed on the rug, useless. He continued his defense, and forced her hands behind her back. "You're mad, feisty as a wild animal." He kissed her ear and nipped at it before forcing her to the bedside. "I could kill you for what you just did. I'd be well within my rights." Pressing his loins against her backside, he, instead, kissed her neck. "Is that what you want?" He kissed again, lowering her face down to the bed. "You want me to kill you?"

His weight pinned her. She wavered between anger at being helpless and the heat that made her want to surrender to his domination. As if he sensed her willingness, he let go of her hands and placed his palms on her waist. She held her words and relaxed. He ground his body into hers, and she wondered what it would feel like to give in to this man, to become whatever he wanted her to be, to please him, to—

"Brother! Quit boffing the help and come down to the meeting. Salak is waiting for us!" A man's voice cut through the mood.

Tolston withdrew, leaving her quavering on the bed. He shook his head when she turned to stare at him. "You wait for me, pretty one. I'll be back tonight. If you need anything, ask Elspeth." He adjusted his clothes, winked at her, and hurried to the door. Opening it wide, he stood there for a moment, a satisfied grin on his handsome, cruel face.

Doran peered around his brother's shape and frowned. "Lady," he said, confusion twisting his face. "Are you all right?"

"She's fine," Tolston grumbled. He strode past his brother, shoving him in the process. His steps echoed down the hall.

Althyn held Doran's gaze as she gathered the bedcover over her nakedness. "I want my servant back...and my uncle. You took my uncle." Her voice held less conviction than it had earlier. She stood from the bed and frowned. "I want them back."

Doran flushed. He turned his head to peek down the hall and then walked timidly into the chamber. "Please, Lady. I gave you money. Go back to where you came from. We only take those that, by rights, should be taken. I know nothing of your uncle, but your slave was marked and belongs to the church. Whoever sold him to you probably stole him. I'm sorry for your loss." He swallowed and took a step closer to her. "And if I may suggest, you shouldn't be here, not with my brother. He's no gentleman."

"So I see." Althyn turned her back on his kindness, unused to it and distrusting him. Her body felt weighted by the encounter with Tolston. She bent to retrieve her ruined dress and tossed it across the bed. Her sword lay on the rug. Kneeling, she retrieved that as well and set it by her dress. "I have nothing else to wear."

Doran ambled closer and wrung his hands. "I can have another dress brought to you and...undergarments. Please, Lady. You must leave."

She traced the hilt of her sword, frowning. "You must let me see them, my uncle and my slave. I need to know they're alive and safe." A burst of emptiness exploded in her mind, and it made her body cold. She contemplated killing the man near her just for spite. *What would Tolston think of me if I did that? He'd fear me then.* A smile curved her lips, and she forced it away.

"I, um, I can take you to see them. If you promise me you'll leave after that." He fidgeted with his sleeve and stared at her.

"Now? Can I see them now?" She slipped her fingers around the hilt of her blade.

He looked her up and down. "Let me make an excuse not to attend the meeting. Salak has more faith in my brother as it is. I won't be missed. Then, I'll get you clothes and we can go to the tower together, but you must promise you'll do as I say."

"I promise," she whispered.

FRESH HAY LAY across the stone floor Althyn and Doran crossed to get to the rear cells of the tower. She wore a cotton dress that fit poorly, but covered her nakedness. Her sword, she'd left in Doran's room after a heated debate. Men catcalled as she passed their cells, some reaching out in an attempt to grasp her skirt.

"Ignore them," Doran told her. "The filth." He wove his fingers with hers and guided her along. His grip was cold and his sincerity unsettling.

At the end of the long hall of prisoners, he stopped and motioned to a man huddled in the corner of a dark cell. A thin ray of sunlight landed before the man's sandaled feet. Althyn's heart skipped. Heat rushed through her, and she didn't understand her strange emotions and doubted if she ever would.

"Lainious?"

He lifted his head, his eyes shadowed still from lack of sleep. He stared at her, dumbstruck. "Mistress, you shouldn't be here."

"You see," Doran expanded. "Even he knows his rightful place. Let me take you back to…well, to where you live. I'll escort you personally and be sure you're safe."

She let go of his hand and fisted the bars. "Lainious, come here. Have they hurt you?"

He shook his head as he stood. "No, mistress. No one's hurt me. It's well that I go back to the church. You've been kind to me, but I'm marked. I've belonged to the Othians since birth. They will care for me well there."

Althyn gritted her teeth. "No. You're mine. You belong to *me*. The crew, they've all gone. The ship is empty. I won't go back there without you."

"Lady, please," Doran interrupted. "Forget the Othian slave. Now, what is your uncle's name so I can check the roster and find him for you? Depending on his crimes, you may be able to post a fee for his release."

Lainious shook his head, his wide eyes warning her not to divulge the information.

"Anthis Laethwyn," she said, her gaze never leaving her servant's face. "And you"—she held her hand out to Lainious while Doran shuffled away to look up the name. Lowering her voice, she said—"you come here to me and show me the church's mark."

He walked slowly, like a defeated man. "There is nothing you can do."

He unlaced his breeches and inched them down to show off the runelike circles and intersecting lines. "You see. It was burned into my skin when I came of age."

"Closer," she ordered and knelt in the hay. Althyn put her hand through the gap in the bars and placed her palm over the mark. He flinched. "I can make it go away."

He placed his hand over hers, his skin warm and dirt-stained. "Mistress, save yourself. When that guard realizes you're related to Arin…when he knows the crimes Anthis and your father committed, they'll throw you in here, too. I beg you to go."

She glanced up at his face. "You belong to *me,* for all time." Gathering the strange energy that hovered in her mind, the mist that lingered when she tried to bend the men's minds to hers, she willed the mark to go away. She wanted everything back the way it was when she'd boarded her father's ship. Events had left her control, and she didn't like it.

The ridges of the scar heated under her touch. Bumps and lines sizzled, then melted. Lainious whimpered, but didn't shy away. When Althyn lifted her chin to check his face, she saw pain and hope there. He no more wanted to return to the church than she wanted him to be taken.

Silvery blue light showed at the edges of her hand and fingers. The heat shifted to cold, and burned like ice left against skin too long. She drew her hand away and grinned. "Mine."

Lainious ran his forefinger over the place where the mark used to be. "Althyn," he whispered. "You need to leave this place. Magic is forbidden."

Doran entered the hall, his pace harried. "Lady, there must be some mistake," he began. "Your uncle is…that is to say, his crimes…"

She stood straight and stared at Doran, sending forth the mist to wrap itself round his mind. He bode her no ill will and felt sorry to have to explain her uncle's circumstances. She found it difficult to control him, something to do with her attraction, or lack thereof, toward him. His soft manner and kindness made revulsion twist in her stomach.

He hesitated, stumbling. His lips parted as he tried to gather his words. She snatched up his hand and pressed a quick kiss to his cheek. His eyes widened.

"Open the cell. This man bears no mark. I demand he be returned to me."

Doran touched his lips. Dazed, he tried to shake her hold. "I-I-I have seen the mark."

"He has none now! You're stealing from me, taking my most precious possessions. Open the cell. I want my property!" She stamped her foot. The other prisoners started yowling and calling, their deep voices filling the chamber.

She reached up and grasped his hair, drawing his face to hers. "You let him out, or I'll kill you and free him myself. I'll *take* what's mine."

Doran froze, trapped in her gaze and unable to comply. But, he also had no effect on her. There was no maddening drive to mate, to press closer to him.

"I can't do that," he finally forced out. "I would do anything else you ask, but not that."

She groaned, frustrated. Her fingernails sank into his scalp, sharpening and hardening into something else. Lainious gasped beside her and took hold of her sleeve, trying to gather her attention.

"Mistress, please, you're changing…your face!"

Chapter Ten
Sister's Wings

PAIN NEEDLED ACROSS her chin. Althyn released Doran and swiped at her skin absently. The softness there startled her. She drew her fingers away. When she opened her mouth to order him again, her sweet voice cracked and sputtered out in a broken, graveled tone. "Release him!"

Doran's eyes bulged. He shook his head, taking harried steps backward to escape her wrath. He stumbled and fell onto the floor. Terrified, he pushed his way across the strewn straw. The prisoners laughed and shouted all manner of foul names.

Ringing sounded in Althyn's ears. She clapped her taloned hands over them to try and make it stop. Her body trembled. As they had beneath the sea, bones shifted and contorted. Two bolts of hot pain burst at her shoulder blades, tearing her dress. Wet heat dribbled down her back.

"Mistress!" Lainious screamed. He, too, backed away, ending up flat against the rear of his cell.

She tried to hold her ruined clothing over her body, but as she grasped the edge of the cloth, her claws sliced through the fabric. Finally, with a high-pitched squawk, she reversed her tactic and forced the garment off.

"The key!" she called.

Doran held his arm over his face and began muttering prayers.

Frustrated and unsure of the strange shape her body was taking, she faced Lainious's prison, took hold of the bars, and pulled. Metal strained and creaked. The iron twisted under her strength. She clenched her mouth only to find she no longer had teeth but a hard, shell-like beak. She wrenched the door to the right and it shuddered, finally breaking free.

Triumphant, she opened her mouth to order Lainious out, but all that escaped her was a harsh cawing sound. Standing upright proved impossible now. She dropped to all fours and sauntered into the cell to retrieve her prize.

Lainious closed his eyes and made a symbol over his heart. Althyn flicked her tail, glanced back to watch its tuft fly this way and that. She hissed. White feathers tipped black arced behind her. She'd changed into her dead sister. This pleased her, although she didn't understand why it had occurred.

She paced, troubled. Doran remained prone outside. The other prisoners had gone silent, save for a few jumbled mumblings. "*Lainious,*" she thought, "*you must come with me or die.*"

He cracked his eyes open and nodded, understanding. "All right, Mistress."

She ruffled her wings and folded them across her back, wondering what it would feel like to fly. Part of her wanted to tear out the wall and leap into the clouds, to soar over the city and disappear from memory. Another part of her yearned to feed, to tear up her servant with her beak and swallow up chunks of his flesh.

Her will hazed over. She fought it, and padded to the wall with its tiny barred window. Grasping the metal, cold and hard in her birdlike hands, she jerked the bars from the mortar and created the beginnings of a hole to escape through. Bits of stone and dust tumbled to the floor. She rose up on her hind legs and leapt at the wall, feral and determined. A massive chunk of stone and mortar broke off and plummeted to the outside world.

Althyn fell with it, spinning through the air. On instinct, she spread her new wings. They caught, forcing her sideways at an awkward angle. Flying was something new and terrible. Squawking, she somersaulted and tried to gain her bearings. Below her, a courtyard spanned. To the east, the pastures and walls. Above, she targeted the ruined tower and the gaping hole she'd created.

Lainious. The thought propelled her forth. Her great wings flapped and made heavy whispers through the air. Her taloned hands curled against her feathered, wide chest. Pressing together her rear legs, she tucked them in to resist the wind.

She clutched the edge of the ruined wall and scrambled back inside. Doran had fled, leaving the door swinging on its hinges. Althyn lunged forth, snatched her ward in one clawed hand, and darted away, wobbling as she became airborne once more.

Her clumsy flight carried her low over the courtyard. She swept her other arm around Lainious' neck, hugging him to her body in an effort to regain her balance. Wingtips grazed treetops. She hissed through her beak at the people shouting below.

She breached the outer wall of the fortress and glided over the pastures. Bleating sheep scattered beneath her shadow, pale puffs against a dark green carpet of grasses. She salivated, hungry, starved, and fighting the desire to drop her servant, dive down and tear up a fresh, wooly chunk of mutton.

Before long, the thick forest swallowed her up. She had no room to maneuver between the trees. Lainious shouted as best he could with his wind being cut off, and she dropped him. Her wings tangled in gnarled branches. Feathers tore free. Flailing her arms and legs, she broke out of the forest's snare and fell in a heap on the ground.

"Mistress?" Lainious crawled toward her. Blood trickled from claw marks on his bare skin where she'd accidentally pierced it. The scent of the dark fluid caused her stomach to rumble. When he reached out his hand to her, she snapped at his fingers. He pulled away in time to save his hand.

I'm so hungry, she thought.

He nodded in understanding before backing to the trees. "Change back. Be what you are."

She shook her head to rid it of the buzzing in her ears. Althyn tugged her wings to her sides and folded them across her back. She flicked her tail and closed her eyes, concentrating. The change was not as easy as becoming a mer in the depths of the sea. She realized this shift had been brought on by her anger. Her hand had changed in the same manner when she'd confronted the crewmember and sliced through his flesh with those same black talons. She steadied her wild breathing.

Bones rearranged. Flesh melted. Feathers dropped from her skin and fell away. Her shape diminished, and she shivered with the onset of chills from stress and the cooler forest air.

She trembled when Lainious stood by her side. He placed a warm hand on her bare shoulder. "Mistress," he whispered, "what *are* you?"

She opened her eyes and glared at him, bitter and frightened of what had happened. "I don't know. I've never really known." Althyn sat back and gathered her knees to her chest. She buried her face there and closed her eyes tight against the tears that threatened. "My mother said I was mermish, of the sea, but this...what I shifted into... I need my uncle. I have to go back."

Lainious gathered her in his arms and pulled her into his lap. "We will get him, Althyn. Rest now. You're shaking so badly. I think you should sleep."

She nodded and curled into his comforting hold. No one had ever held her like this, save her mother. She didn't like it, but her quaking body warned her not to resist. Dizziness set in. The peculiar ringing in her ears had vanished when she had changed back to her true shape. She heard his heart beating so fast. Time wore on while she focused on the steadying rhythm. The haze set in over her mind, but combined with the weariness from shifting, she hardly felt its euphoric effects until she lifted her face to stare at him.

"Lainious, I left my mother's – *my* sword in there. I have to get it back. I shouldn't be sitting here in the middle of the woods."

He combed his fingers through her hair and shushed her. "Rest a little while. I wish I had a blanket or something to cover you." He rubbed her upper arm with one hand, trying to warm her.

She frowned at him. "Why are you so kind to me?"

His deep blue eyes held her gaze. The gray mist clouded in his eyes and all around them. Her heart thumped hard. His mouth pleased her. The high guard had awakened something she didn't understand. Her body stirred, and she pressed her bare chest to his, her mouth flush with his lips.

"You have not treated me ill," he answered, his voice fading. "And you stole me from the fortress. You took me from the tower. No master or mistress has ever done such a thing for me."

She liked the way his soft lips felt, moving against hers when he spoke. His gentle nature soothed her, although she longed for a fight. In fact, her body screamed for a battle. This time, she closed her eyes and gave in to the pulsing maelstrom of energy sparking between them. Althyn kissed her servant gently and willed him to return her attentions, not that he needed any urging. His heat warmed her cold skin. His body fit to hers when he lay to one side and held her close. His strong arms encircled her.

"Please," he began when she paused to breathe. "I don't deserve these attentions from you. I am nothing." His desire showed in his gaze as well as the crush of his body next to hers.

She marveled at how he could say such things. Men took what they wanted and felt no guilt. Well, most men. Those who didn't were weak. She wriggled her toes and frowned. "My sandals were destroyed in the tower."

"I will make you another pair." He leaned in and kissed her cheek. "As many sandals as you want."

She smiled and curled into him, hoping the euphoria of closeness they shared would ease the weakness she currently suffered. Her trembling had subsided, but she didn't think she could walk just yet, much less shift her shape. "I looked like a gryphon, didn't I?"

"Yes, mistress. Just like the one you had me sew into your flag."

Chapter Eleven
Call of the Sea

LEAVES CLUNG TO her bare skin when Althyn stood. Lainious slept on the forest floor, his eyes moving behind closed lids. She stared at his body, at his worn pants and dirt-stained fingers. She decided her servant should not go about looking so ill-treated.

Naked and refreshed from having rested, she brushed away the traces of sleeping in the open. She glanced around the woods at the fog clinging to the ground. Sighing, she ran her fingers through her hair and longed for her mirror.

"Mistress?" Lainious mumbled.

She looked down and frowned when he reached for her and his hand met the emptiness. He blinked and sat up. Squinting, he visibly eased when he realized she hadn't gone far. Blood had crusted over his skin where she'd clawed him during their escape. She sat back beside him and reached to touch the wounds with tentative fingers. "I hurt you."

He placed his hand over hers and shook his head. "It's all right. I will heal in time."

"My mother used to sing after my father left. She had a beautiful voice. I could listen to her long into the night while she held herself in her bed and rocked back and forth." Althyn closed her eyes, envisioning her mother's shadow swaying across the floor.

She pressed her hand hard against Lainious's wounds and sang the same words she'd memorized. He flinched, but didn't withdraw. A wave of pulsing heat settled in around her mind. She knew if she opened her eyes, she'd long to kiss him as she had the night before. It wasn't what she wanted. Althyn only desired to mend what she had broken. Her mother's words never healed anything, but Althyn knew, she understood at that moment why.

She chose him. It made sense now. She'd thought her mother had been human until the day she died. By then, Yneria *was* human. She'd abandoned her mermish lineage and forsaken her magic for the love of an elf who'd beaten her. "What a waste," she blurted when the song ended.

A sweet dizziness settled over her mind. She swayed forward only to have her servant catch her and hold her steady. "By Othia, Althyn. You're a healer."

She cracked her weary eyes open to stare at his mended skin. "Yes. Apparently, I am many things. The question is, what limits do I have?"

"Thank you," he said and gathered her body to his. "My mistress, you are a treasure beyond words."

She merely shook her head and pouted. "Just take me to my ship. I need to hear the ocean, see the waves and eat, maybe rest. I'm tired again."

THE VOICES CALLED her name. How they knew it, she couldn't guess, but it did sound sweet and alluring as it drifted through the hull of the ship. Each tenor bounced from the wooden walls. Each basso rumbled and tore at her heart. Althyn tossed and turned, her mind awakening, her body tense. She smelled them, salty, musky creatures. They were a part of her. She needed to find them, to touch them, to join them. Their music promised her a home, a place to belong. She longed for such pure acceptance.

Lainious sat on the bed beside her and touched her forehead. "Your fever is gone. I've made you some fish soup. Sit up and I'll help you drink the broth." His eyes no longer had darkness beneath them.

The music she thought she'd dreamed continued to sway and gather around her mind. Her stomach grumbled. She scooted back and sat up. "Do you hear them?"

Lainious looked at her curiously. "Hear who?"

"The voices. The singing voices." She pushed her blanket away, suddenly hot. At some point, he'd dressed her in a sleeping shift. Althyn picked at the light fabric. "Can't you hear them?"

"I only hear the sea." He took a bowl from the tray at her bedside table and lifted it to her lips. "Drink, mistress. You've been asleep all day."

She snarled. "Why didn't you wake me?" Her hand rose reflexively to slap him, but he cowered and lowered the bowl without spilling a drop. She felt the twinge of change tracing her skin, threatening to shift her shape without her approval. His subservient gaze stopped her. Sucking in slow, calming breaths, she halted the shift.

"I tried." He glanced up, his gaze piercing her. "Believe me, I did."

She took the bowl from his hands. Drinking down the thin broth, she listened. Waves slapped at the side of the ship. People's voices drifted on the breeze from the docks. The mer had stopped singing. Althyn drank all of the soup. She held the empty bowl out to Lainious.

He took it and set it aside. "I've word about your uncle, more specifically about you. The High Guard is searching for you. There's a price on your head."

She pushed off the bed and padded across the planks. "High Guard? Which one?" The thought of Tolston caused her to blush, heat racing up her neck and cheeks.

"The dark-haired one. He claims you stole something from his room. Lies, all of it, I know, but that doesn't matter. Mistress, your uncle is to be hung tomorrow at midday."

A new voice drifted to her, cold and nearly forgotten from the chest at the foot of the bed. "*Release me.*"

"Be silent!" she spat.

"Yes, as you wish." Lainious took the tray and left the room, misunderstanding her.

Althyn leaned against the wall and stared at her reflection in the mirror. "Midday," she whispered. Different ideas twirled in her mind. She could go to the High Guard and demand her uncle back. She could shift and pluck Anthis from the noose before his time. None of it seemed plausible. Her father's voice muttered and grumbled from its prison in the axe. She raised an eyebrow, wondering if the axe wasn't such a bad option.

A single, feminine song drifted into the chamber. The boat swayed in gentle motion with the tide. Frustrated, Althyn left her room and climbed the stairs. Lainious sat cross-legged on the deck, his back to her. A pile of netting lay in a heap at his side. He was knotting and mending in silence. She padded toward him, drawn to the lure of his bare skin. Moonlight glanced off the scars over his back.

"Sister," a voice hissed. "Sister, come to us."

She reached for Lainious and halted, contemplating why she felt so drawn to him at times and yet so repulsed by his subservience at others. Her outstretched hand returned to her side. Althyn tugged off the shift she wore and let it fall to the deck. The wind picked up, rustling the rolled sails high above. She traced a finger down the center of her chest and turned from her servant to look over the ship's side.

Squinting, she waited, hopeful. The waves rippled and churned, much as her emotions. She bent over and caught sight of something below the surface, a silhouette bleached a faded blue by the night colors. The thing emerged from the sea, bearing a woman's face. Her cheeks glittered with moisture, or what might be scales.

"Sister," it said, and held out beckoning arms. "You belong with us, not here, not among the land walkers. Come."

Althyn ran a hand through her hair. She glanced over her shoulder at Lainious. Oblivious to her, he remained hunched over, his long fingers continuing to work at the netting. His bare chest called to her, but the mer just below said nothing and the lure of familial ties, if indeed that's what they were, caused her to climb over the railing and leap into the sea's soothing embrace.

Once below the waves, she allowed her body to change. Air fled her lungs in great, silver bubbles. The mermaid circled Althyn, swimming in and out of the clouds of blood brought on by the shift. Bones knitted. Muscles tore and grew to suit her ancestors' shape. With a flick of her tail, Althyn swam after the one who had beckoned her. She was a silvery green creature of beauty.

"*Lotias knows of you. Thenai and Sherak as well. Where is your mother, little one? Has she learned the error of her ways?*" The mermaid's eyes were two inky pools of mesmerizing darkness. She slowed her pace and hung limp in the water, regarding Althyn.

"*My mother is dead, killed by my father.*" She pushed away floating locks of her own hair when they drifted in her view. "*I know nothing of those you speak about.*" Reaching, she touched the mermaid on her shoulder. Her skin felt cold as ice.

The mermaid smiled, revealing double fangs. "*Of course. You know naught of your race. Come. Follow me to the center of the underworld, and I will teach you. Lotias will want you. He will.*" She also touched Althyn in turn, her icy fingers stroking her cheek. "*You have your mother's face.*" Those same icy fingers quested higher and sought out the shape of Althyn's ear. "*Ah, and the mark of your father. A shame.*"

Althyn backed away. "*Where are these others you tell me of? How far?*"

The mermaid turned her attention to the darkness beyond and waved a delicate hand out to sea. "*Just there. Not far. Come. I'll take you to them. You will know others like you.*" She swished her powerful tail and started in the direction she'd indicated, her body a shimmer of light darting away.

Althyn glanced at the hull of her ship and frowned. Midday. It was night, and she had to be at the hold to gather her uncle by the sun's highest point. She wondered if Lainious would miss her if she didn't return, or if it was better to let her uncle go in exchange for this new life. Frowning, she twisted and slapped her tail at the current, hurrying to catch up to the mermaid.

"*What do I call you?*" she thought as she swam at a faster pace. She made time with the mermaid, her eyes ahead, her heart swelling at the prospect of finding other mers.

"*Shael. I am not of your kin.*" The mermaid stole a long stare at Althyn, her small lips curving. "*Oh no, not of your line at all.*" Shadows played about them, slithering shapes with fishlike grace. They circled and closed in.

Althyn's heart pounded in her chest. Her mind rushed with emotions, excitement, hope…and as the figures emerged and their visages became clear, a new emotion riddled her—fear.

The males of the mer were not much to look upon. Great, hulking beings, the three of them appraised Althyn, their beards swaying in the water. Seaweed and creatures lurked in those same beards. Their green hair glowed in the shots of moonlight filtering from the surface. She didn't like the way they looked upon her. It was not the same lost gaze the land walker males suffered. These males, with their wide chests and pupil-free black eyes watched her with bitterness. Their brows rumpled and they uncurled their thick fingers, baring daggerlike blue claws.

Chapter Twelve
Servant's Touch

"THIS IS THE princess?" the largest male asked, his voice echoing in Althyn's mind. He lunged forward, grasped a fistful of her hair and yanked her toward him. *"I claim her. She is mine."* The cold, firm skin of his chest crushed into her breasts. She stared into his eyes and fear turned, like it so often did of late, into a bitter anger. Her eyes narrowed into slits. She opened her fingers and willed talons to lengthen.

Another male twisted his tail and approached. *"She should be mine."*

The mermaid watched, intent, spinning around the gathering with a feral grin before she vanished in the darkness of the depths.

Althyn grasped the waist of the male who held her and dug her talons into his flesh. Blood clouded the water around them. His emotionless eyes seemed to focus on her. Slowly, his hold on her wrist weakened, and she slapped her tail in an attempt to escape.

The other male darted in, his hands outstretched to stake his claim.

She spun and slashed, missing him and forcing her body up toward the surface. The shape of the moon, distorted by waves, was like a target above. She needed to escape this side of her. Fingers curled over her shoulders, drawing her backward. Althyn opened her mouth to scream her rage as the third merman's hand slicked down her arms then and fastened over her misshapen hands, holding her steady. His eyes were not the same as the others', but a sea green, calm and hypnotic.

"*My princess,*" he said in her mind. "*You must return to your people. Your grandfather is dead and without your mother to take his place, there is chaos in the underworld. The others would claim you and steal your throne.*"

"*Throne?*" She jerked her arms, but couldn't pull free from his steely hold. "*My place is not here, not with your kind. You're hideous, all of you.*"

Her insult caused his mouth to twist into an angered frown. The merman moved closer, his face aligned with hers. Their noses touched and a wave of dizziness affected her. He nuzzled the side of her face, his thoughts dancing in her mind, wordless, full of an unbearable pain, a loneliness she, too, held inside.

His hold became gentle, changing as he slipped his arms around her waist and swam, spinning them together. Her hair drifted around her face as did his. His beard, less wild than the others, evidenced his youth.

"*I pledge myself to you,*" he swore before he rested his cheek beside hers. Ever faster they whirled through the water until Althyn became dizzy and closed her eyes, relenting to the merman's hold. She plied against his body, their tails flapping in unison, his mind and hers, melding.

"*What do I call you?*" she questioned.

"*I am Sherak. We are cousins, you and I. Cousins from your mother's line.*" He smiled as they slowed their aquatic dance.

"*If you leave us, Althyn, all will be lost. Please stay. Stay here with me.*"

She flinched when he caressed her cheek. The water around them calmed, and they stopped near a coral reef. Floating in his embrace, she studied him. "*Can you walk upon the land with me?*"

His face tightened. Finally, after a long period of silent contemplation, Sherak nodded once. His fingers entwined with hers. Together, they swam to the surface, breaching it to breathe in the air. The green of his skin paled to a more human shade. They waded to the shore, their scales sloughing off like silvery coins across the froth. Side by side, naked and walking on two feet, both emerged to stroll along the wet sand.

"I have never done this before," he said. "The others would demean me for this betrayal."

She had a thousand questions to ask before this moment, but none came. "The lord will hang my uncle tomorrow," she blurted.

"Then it is good. You will have nothing left to hold you to this world." He faced her, the sea at his back, the moon glowing beyond. "There are those in need of a leader, a powerful mage like your grandfather. Let the man of your father's line die. You have no need of anything other than what the waves provide." He held her hand to his lips as if to kiss it, but instead, ran it across his lips.

His body offered no heat like that of a man's or an elf's. Althyn didn't like the cold of the merman, but his eyes and his words intrigued her. She pulled her hand away and frowned. "I must go back to my ship."

"Your father's ship," he corrected.

"My father is dead. I killed him. And if you or any of your kind stand in my way, make no mistake. I'll kill you too."

He smiled at her, his teeth sharp and dangerous. "I believe you." Sherak took a step backward. "If you have need of me…if you have want for the wind in your sails, as well, all you must do is ask the sea."

"I have need of my uncle."

The merman smirked. "I would expect a princess such as yourself to take what is rightfully hers. Don't you understand what you are?"

She glowered at him. He had asked the one question she couldn't answer. Seeking her true nature was a never ending quest of secrets that led to more mysteries. "No," she whispered, angry that she didn't know, livid that he seemed to know and flaunted his knowledge.

His greenish-black eyebrows drew together. He glanced over his shoulder for a moment. Turning back, he said, "Althyn, you are your mother's daughter. You are the most coveted and last descendant of King Elthian. The sea will answer your bidding, as will the sky, the rivers, and any body of water. They are yours to command. Don't let the others control you." He backed further until the surf bubbled over his bare feet. "Don't believe them…"

"Sherak," she whispered, holding a hand out for him to return to.

"Sing for me if you would have me as your mate. Call for me if you need the aid of an army at sea. I would never hold you to me and force you as the others tried."

He stepped into the waves, his body reshaping itself. With a splash from his green tail, her cousin, if that's who he really was, returned whence he'd come, leaving her as alone as ever.

Naked, she walked along the shore humming to herself.

It was late into the night. No one was about to leer and gawk at her nudity when she crossed the dock to her ship. Lainious was asleep across his nets. Her nightdress clung to a mast, fluttering in the cool breeze. She pulled it on and covered herself.

"Lainious," she said, shaking his shoulder. "Come to bed now. It's late, and we've a long day ahead of us."

He blinked up at her, dazed.

"Mistress, I can sleep here."

She shook her head. "Come to bed now…with me."

"I can't sleep in your bed, Althyn."

"You can and you will."

He nodded and stood. She took hold of his hand and pulled him along, impatient and unsettled by all that had happened. When she got into bed and lay beside her servant, he touched her moist hair.

"Were you swimming?"

"Yes. Don't ask any more questions." She covered his mouth with hers, bringing on the euphoria she wanted to lose herself in. At first, he resisted, balking until she took hold of the back of his head and forced him to hold still. His eyes soon slipped shut. His lips parted, and she tasted his mouth, testing his tongue as Tolston had done to her. Althyn's body came alive. Her breasts felt full; her nipples hardened to an uncomfortable degree. Between her legs, moisture crept in.

"Mistress," he whispered, trembling, "why me? Why do you show this affection to me?"

"Because you're here," she answered, and at once knew the coldness and truth of her words. "I can't help myself. I feel this drive, this lust to…" She knew what her body craved. She had come of age, and instinct demanded a mate. The thought of giving herself over to any one male disturbed her. Lainious wasn't a threat, though. He was hardly a man at all.

He closed his mouth, his lower lip sticking out in a small pout for a time. "You have never lain with a man."

"No. Never."

"I have not..." He sighed. "If you're in need of a teacher, of a man with experience in such matters..."

She giggled at him. "What a pair we make. A virgin slave in the bed of a virgin mistress."

He chewed his lip for a moment, his eyes brightening. "I have seen it done, if you want me to try."

Althyn grimaced. "I have seen it done, as well. A sight I'd sooner like to forget."

"Oh." He frowned.

A rush of heat spread through her body, tangling up her thoughts. Lainious's eyes glossed over as they so often did when she came close to him. Althyn wrapped her arms around him and touched the thick scars across his back. "I wish I could erase all my father has done." She hummed her mother's song under her breath, drawing her fingertips down each scar, willing them to become only memory. His old wounds obeyed, skin smoothing and reshaping at her urging.

"It tingles when you touch me that way," he managed to push the words out.

She nodded and finished the healing. Fatigue threatened, and she moved in to kiss his mouth until she was too tired to go on.

"Tomorrow, I take back my uncle, and my sword," she slurred. His lips trailed over her cheek in soft, wet caresses. She wanted them to be firm, needed him to dominate her, but he only explored with an inexperienced ease, down her neck and grazing her skin above her gown.

Althyn reached beneath the covers to his crotch and discovered the same hardness there as Tolston had. She cupped that part of his body and rubbed it in slow strokes.

Lainious moaned against her skin.

The longer she massaged his manhood, the weaker he became until he shuddered and cried her name against her breasts. His breeches warmed with moisture. She pulled her hand away and clutched him to her body, understanding a little more about the workings of males.

"I'm sorry." He snuggled closer to her, his strong arms cinched around her waist, his face pressed to her chest.

She found herself wishing he would pull away her clothes and taste her body, or at least run kisses over her breasts. They burned for attention. When he began to snore, she groaned her frustration and tried to get some sleep. The following day would be long and full of trials. She supposed she ought to prepare for it as best she could. The pull to claim a mate annoyed her. It made her want things she knew she should not; it gave her a sense of why her mother had made such a foul choice. Althyn didn't want to follow in her mother's path.

Chapter Thirteen
Plotting

SHE DREAMED OF Sherak, of the coolness of his skin when he touched his body to hers. In her vision, they coupled on the beach in human form, their bodies dotted with sweat, their fingers knotting in each others' hair and his kisses urgent, painful with the sharpness of his teeth. She bucked to meet the pounding of his body and suddenly awoke, feverish and unsated, with Lainious by her side still asleep. Althyn wondered if Sherak had sent her the dream, for she had never had night visions of that ilk.

She stared at her servant, the hunger and lust of her dream still fresh. Althyn pulled him closer until he lay upon his back. He muttered incoherent words. She climbed atop him, tugged down his breeches and investigated the shape of his body. The place where he'd been marked was smooth and free of damage now, but lower, across the insides of his thighs, more brands twisted and turned, more markings of the Othian Church. She clenched her teeth, angry that someone else had dared damage her property like this. It didn't matter that he hadn't been hers then.

She slipped her hands between his legs and palmed the raised brands, willing them with her song and her magic to blend away and be gone. Lainious's head lolled from side to side. Althyn watched him, her body heated and aroused. Above the places she healed, his manhood stiffened as he, too, became affected by her contact. His blue eyes flickered before he finally stared at her with a questioning expression.

"Mistress?" he whispered.

She plucked the ties open at her bodice and pulled away the nightdress. "Be silent."

His throat clicked. His eyes went glassy and empty.

With the desire to mate came the overwhelming urge to cause pain, to wound, or even kill him. She tried to shake away that desire, but it lingered and grew. Althyn crawled across his body and settled atop her servant. She swayed from side to side, experiencing the feel of his skin against hers, his heat, so unlike the merman she had been close to the night before. The delicious warmth of men drowned out the coldness she felt growing inside her.

She parted her legs, aligning their bodies. His heat increased. She heard the sound of his heart hammering in his chest. The thrill of domination surged through her. She took hold of his hands and forced them above his head, pinning him in place.

He let out a startled cry that echoed in the chamber. "Althyn..." His voice trailed away.

She rolled her hips, tempted to end the drive to claim him—to claim any male. That it didn't matter who it was that she took, disturbed her. It made no difference to her body whether it be this poor, broken slave or the high guard in the keep. She wriggled and bucked, but hesitated when the head of his sex settled at her entry.

He whimpered when she reached into his mind to find that his thoughts were empty, wiped clean by her control.

"Take me, Lainious," she ordered in a soft moan. "I need you to force me, to command me."

His lips parted in a rounded expression of wonder. "Mistress, please, I can't do what you ask."

She groaned and lunged for his mouth, kissing him hard with pent up hunger. He made a small cry in the back of his throat. His fears ran through her, his desire as well. He wanted her in the same way, but something held him back from claiming what she offered. She ravaged his mouth, the heat building between them.

Her lips and tongue took in his cheek, journeyed to his neck, and she sucked his skin into her mouth, nipping it with her teeth. Fangs had lengthened during this dark process and when they pierced his skin, he flinched, escaping her.

"Please," he begged, "don't do this to me. Not me, Althyn."

Angered, she pushed away from him and rolled off the bed. She tightened her hands into fists while she paced at the foot of the bed, pausing every so often to glare his way. "I want it to stop!"

He reached down to pull up his breeches and cover his nakedness. After twisting off the bed, he stood. Lainious edged along the wall, avoiding her. "I'll go and tend to the chores on deck."

She chased after him and shoved him against the wall. Her fingers latched to his shoulders. "What's happening to me? Why am I like this?"

He shook his head.

"I can't think straight. Even my dreams are poisoned with lust. I want a man to mate with me, to use my body, to make this burning desire go away. Can you do this thing? Can you do this for me?"

"All right. I'll try to help you." His hands settled on her bare hips before he lowered his body and knelt before her.

He looked up, his face guilty. "I won't hurt you," he said, "but I won't take what you should only offer to a husband."

He closed his eyes and buried his face against the blonde curls of her mound. She parted her legs to let his tongue linger in rolling waves over her tender skin. His hands held fast to her ankles while he tasted her. The heat peaked in her center until she reached down to hold his bobbing head. It felt like a sweet pain, a seething ripple of sensation. She groaned and struggled to hold still while her body tensed and released. The pent up drive in her pulsed away with each contraction inside her womb. She sank to her knees and held his face to her chest, panting.

"You must never leave me, Lainious."

He nodded, his face lowered as if in shame. "I will stay at your side as long as you find use in me. I swear my loyalty to you, always."

LATER THAT MORNING, he brought a bucket of heated water and washed her body with a clean rag. Lainious helped Althyn to dress in finery from her mother's box of treasures, and he stood at her back, plaiting her hair while she looked at the mirror. "You must stay here on the ship so I know you're safe," she advised. "I will go to the lord's keep alone and face the high guard."

She watched his mouth tense as if he wanted to protest, but he remained silent. Althyn decided she liked that about him and that, if all men in her presence acted in such a way when she wanted silence, it would please her.

"I will take my father's axe."

"How will you hide it?"

She glared. "I will hide nothing." She straightened the skirt she wore and stood after he had finished her hair. "I will walk into the crowd with my axe and cleave off the head of any man who stands in my way." She knelt at the chest and reached in for the enchanted weapon. Her father's voice cursed her from within the confines of wood and metal. She lifted the axe out, ignoring his soul.

"Clean yourself up, Lainious. Be ready to set sail by sunset."

"Yes, mistress," he muttered, and left her chamber to tend to the chores of his station.

Althyn slipped the axe into its casing and shouldered the weapon. Its weight centered between her shoulders. A swell of hatred, bitterness and anger billowed in her mind. She glanced at herself a final time in the looking glass, pleased by her grim, fierce expression. In a way, she looked like her father, and that suited her. His wrath belonged on this mission, not the softness of her mother or the sensual need to couple that had overwhelmed her before Lainious's ministrations. Now she needed to be strong, ruthless.

She left her father's ship, crossed the docks, and wended her way through the masses and the market. Her passing drew many a man's wandering eyes. She wore no veil and swore never to do so again. She was what she was and refused to hide it. Let them stare. Let them long for her.

At the gate to the keep, she passed through with a mass of curiosity seekers who had come to watch the hangings. At the head of the crowd, a gallows loomed with a line of criminals at its flank, all hooded and shackled.

High Guard Tolston stood on the stage, his arms crossed over his chest, his face set and serious while the executioner hauled up the first man to die. Another man read off crimes while a noose tightened about the prisoner's neck. With swift abandon, the executioner rolled back the handle to drop the door, sending the doomed man falling.

The crack of his neck made Althyn shiver.

She had listened, though. This was not her uncle. Searching the hooded prisoners, she caught sight of

Anthis's greasy black hair hanging from beneath the burlap fabric. Third in line, he fidgeted with his bonds.

"Tolston!" Althyn screeched over the din of the crowd.

The high guard scanned the gathered people, a cocky grin breaking his stern expression when their eyes locked. He elbowed the executioner, and the burly man went to fetch Althyn's uncle from the line as if to hurry along his demise.

"Let the woman through!" Tolston ordered, pointing at her.

The crowd parted, and she strode forth, her father's cruelty burgeoning in her veins. Her anger seemed to feed the vile thing in the axe. Reaching back, she pulled the weapon from its bonds. With both hands, she braced herself, ready to fight.

Tolston laughed.

The crowd echoed him, although their guffaws were less sarcastic. She sensed their curiosity over the promise of a new show. Bloodlust lingered in their thoughts.

"What will you do with that, pretty one?" the high guard taunted. "Bad enough you dropped your sword at my feet."

"Give me back what you stole from me, or I'll kill you."

He cackled with unfounded mirth. "You entertain me." He drew a blade from his back, the same long sword she had left behind. It glinted in the bright sunlight, blinding her for a moment. "If you want a parry, step up and show me what practice you have taking on a *man*."

She climbed the steps to the stage, her uncle near, a noose slipping round his neck. She wanted to speak to him, but didn't dare take her attention from the high guard's cold eyes.

"That sword belongs to me. I will have it back now."

He chuckled. "I thought it was a gift for me, a trophy to profess your love."

Men in the crowd shouted jeers, but she ignored them. "I am incapable of love and if you continue to press me, you will be incapable of the lust you so enjoy."

One of his dark eyebrows rose high. His eyes sparkled with challenge. "Really?" He waved the sword between them in attempt to make her retreat. "Your courage intrigues me, pretty one, as does the bulge of your bosom."

She swung the axe.

He blocked with her sword.

Metal grated and strained.

Althyn glared into Tolston's brown eyes, filled with hatred and devoid of the attraction she'd felt for him before. She wanted him dead, wanted to tear his foul body apart.

He took a step back.

She lunged forward.

The crowd of onlookers cheered them on.

Through clenched teeth she growled, "That sword is mine."

The blade glowed blue. Cool air rushed around them. Strands of Tolston's hair stuck to his face. Sweat trickled down his forehead only to freeze in place. She threw her weight into him just as her sword slid from his grip. With a scream of fury, Althyn and Tolston fell from the stage, careening sideways until they crashed onto the ground below. He had hold of the axe's handle and tried to wrench it free in a vicious tug-of-war.

Tolston rolled her beneath him, bent into her face and smothered her with a lusty kiss. She bit his bottom lip. His blood entered her mouth, and she spat it in his face. "Bastard!" she raged.

Hands gripped her body, pulling Althyn away from her target. She yelled, kicked, screamed and fought, but there were too many of them. Tolston lay on the ground, his face contorting with confusion, the splatters of blood tainting his skin, and his lip bleeding where she'd bitten him. He sat up and examined the axe he held.

"What would you have us do with her, sir?" a man asked.

Tolston raised his face, staring through Althyn. "Take her…to my room."

A cloth stifled her breathing, held in place with a firm, masculine hand. Althyn blinked through the haze settling over her vision. "*I have failed you, Uncle,*" she sent the thought to Anthis. She couldn't see him, or much of anything.

Chapter Fourteen
A Mate

ALTHYN'S BODY SWAYED, and she slipped into a gray darkness where even her thoughts jumbled together. She lingered there, angry and confused until a sharp voice spoke at her side.

"So, witch, you want me dead and here you are again in my chamber."

She opened her eyes to find Tolston sneering at her. He wore no shirt this time, his chest well-muscled and scarred in places. Althyn tried to sit up, but pain shot through her skull. "You bastard," she muttered. "You killed my uncle."

He grinned. "He's back in the tower. I used him to get you here with me. You're a strange one, you are, stealing back your Othian slave and mesmerizing my stupid brother into thinking he saw some magical beast. I can't explain the hole in the cell wall, though. Did you do that, pretty one?"

She turned her head. The wall of weapons held both her axe and long sword among its displayed treasures. "I don't know what you're blabbering about," she lied. "I only want my uncle back. He's all I have left."

His hot fingers closed over hers as he leaned down to peer at her face. "I'll give your uncle his freedom if you let me have my way with you."

She narrowed her eyes. "I'll let you have nothing and kill you soon enough."

Tolston climbed atop the bed and crushed her beneath his weight. His hands laced with hers and forced them down into the pillow at either side of her face. "I'll take what I want then. What do you think of that?" One eyebrow quirked in challenge.

She liked how sure he was of himself, how cocky and forceful. But Althyn only admired his qualities because she desired them for herself. "I think you're about to get what you deserve," she whispered, the heat of his closeness affecting her body. Tingles rippled through her in waves. Her nipples peaked, and wetness slicked between her legs. Here was a man who challenged her. Here was both an opponent and, perhaps, if he survived…a mate.

She lifted her face and nipped at the sore place on his lower lip to remind him of what she'd done. To her surprise, he kissed back, his blood tainting her lips, his tongue invasive. Their kisses became torrid and dangerous. Her fingers squeezed into his until he groaned a whimper of pain in the back of his throat. This pleased her and urged her to do more. She wanted to hurt him, to hear him scream and see fear in his cold, dark eyes.

Tolston's hips began an erotic rhythm atop her. His bulging crotch poked at the apex of her legs. She, too, urged her body to meet his advances.

"Minx," he muttered. "You slutty woman. You know you want me. Your body is begging for it."

Summoning the strange magic that surged in her body, she forced her weight against him, pushing his body off. Fingers still knotted together, they both fell over the side of the bed. His look of shock made her smile.

"How the—"

She kissed his mouth with a violence long buried in her innocence and only now surfacing...like her true nature. Althyn pinned Tolston's hands over his head and assaulted his mouth, her hips grinding down, her body alive with need and anger.

Beneath her, he struggled to keep pace with her passion. When he began to moan, she pulled back, her chin and lips sore from the sharpness of his beard. "You're mine," she growled, her teeth clenched. "Forever."

His face, so full of confused bliss, spurred her on. She reached over to the wall of weapons, took hold of a dagger and waved it at him. "Say it! Say you're mine!"

"What are you?" he asked. "You puzzle me."

She slipped the blade into his pants and sliced downward as she climbed off of him. Shredding his breeches, she exposed his nakedness, his arousal, his weakness. The edge of the blade scraped against his inner thigh. His eyes held hers, a wave of dizziness settling in. "I should cut away this part of you...mark you forever...ruin you...'

He sucked in a breath. His upper lip curled. "Do it, if you think you can, and you'll never know what I could have pleasured you with."

The dagger wedged between his thighs. "You don't think I have the courage?"

He sneered. "Like all women, you'll pass out at the sight of my blood."

She pushed.

He flinched, his eyes widening.

"Don't press me."

"Woman, I think you might be a demoness." He snapped his wrist through the air and sat up in one fluid motion, tugging her hand away.

Althyn grinned. "If I am, you are my consort. A lowly one for me to crush beneath my feet when I'm in a foul mood."

He thrust his hips at her. "I should have stripped off your dress while you slept and taken you then."

With her free hand, Althyn reached down and tugged away her skirt. Their naked bodies aligned, rubbing and wet in the heat of their strange courtship. She dug down further between them, grasped his length and squeezed.

"Damn you, minx," he hissed in pain.

In one fateful, crushing motion, she slammed her hips down and forced his body inside hers. A swift pain erupted inside her, followed by a thick feeling of being filled. She took her hand away, shifting from side to side as he impaled her.

It was done, and she wasn't sure why she'd allowed things to go so far. She had chosen her mate, a foul man very much like her father—tainted, cruel, brash, and handsome. As his fingers found purchase on her hips and he slammed himself inside her body, Althyn closed her eyes, arched her back and let the tides of ecstasy wash over her mind.

They rutted on the floor like beasts, like she'd seen her parents do time and again. She couldn't get enough of him, taking his hand and guiding him to her entrance to pleasure her with his fingers when his manhood would not rise fast enough. He obliged with a snarling grin, lascivious and voracious in his attentions. His tongue and mouth explored every inch of her skin, ever curve, every fold until, by dawn, both of them lay side by side on the rug, sheathed in a sheen of sweat.

"You're evil, woman," Tolston told her, and Althyn knew his words to be true. She was not a shrinking creature meant to stand aside and let a male rule her. She was not a woman like the others she'd seen in the village. She was a force, a power, a surging vessel of need.

When his breathing went steady and he started to snore, she stood, glaring down at him. His body was pleasant to look upon, well-muscled, rugged, and scarred. She imagined she could stand there and stare at him all day, despite the ache in her thighs and the soreness where he'd been inside her. She liked that soreness most of all and wanted it again, many more times.

She also wanted her uncle back.

Sweeping her hair off her shoulders, Althyn went to the wardrobe against the far wall and rifled through it. She stole Tolston's pants and shirt, not the fanciful garb he wore here at the keep, but the plainer works for fighting and patrolling. She braided her hair and tied it with a bit of lacing from one of his shirts.

Full of promise and having had a taste of domination, she took down her father's axe from Tolston's wall, slung it across her back, and waited a moment to accustom herself to the weight of the weapon as well as the burden of the soul trapped within. Next, she took down as many daggers as she could fit on her person, stealing some away in the waist of her pants. Her long sword came last, as light as ever and more tempting now to use for its intended purpose. She imagined holding it aloft and smiting off her mate's head. The blood would spread across the fine rug he rested upon and he would never be able to take another mate. She would be his last.

She shook her head, suddenly troubled with the horrific image her mind so easily created. Swallowing her voice and her strange thoughts, she left Tolston's chamber, bent on getting Anthis back.

"If I can leave Tolston," she said to herself, "then the curse is broken. I can go anywhere, do anything without the burden of my chosen mate."

She skulked through the dark hall, wondering if she could find the tower without anyone's aid. No one hindered her as she passed the closed doors and made her way down the same path Tolston's brother had taken her before. The door to the tower was not guarded, but it was locked. She frowned over this deterrent, but stepped back and took off the axe.

Holding the handle in her hands brought a rush of cruelty to bubble inside her. She swung, slamming the blade into the flesh of the wooden door. Again and again, she attacked the barrier, drawing shouts of confusion from the prisoners within. When the handle and iron lock fell at her feet in a midst of splintered wood, she laughed.

"Anthis!" she shouted, pushing her way inside the tower.

Men called for her to come to them. But she paced along the rows of cells until, at last, she found who she sought.

Her uncle stood at the gate of his prison, his fingers clutched around the bars. "My lass," he said in shock. "I thought he'd have killed you or much worse…"

Shifting her hands into the gryphon's shape, she took hold of the gate and wrenched it free. Anthis gasped at her change, but held his tongue, though she sensed the fear and wonder in his eyes.

"I want to kill the lord," she told him. "Pilfer his coffers and take his wealth as my own. After that, I want to go to the Othian Church."

Anthis choked and sputtered. "What are you saying?"

She raised a hand, ready to slap his face.

He stepped back into the shadows of his cell.

"You heard me, Uncle." She lowered her taloned hand and willed it to return to its usual shape. "I want to take the Othian Dagger, the relic my father wasn't good enough to steal." A shiver ran down her spine, a tempting hint of passion that lingered after her coupling with the high guard. She wanted him again. She fought the urge and stomped out of the tower, not bothering to look back and see if Anthis followed.

Like a predator, she stalked through the keep. Her senses heightened so that she smelled each and every living thing within the chambers. She heard heartbeats and breathing, tasted the flavor of men and women in the air. Entering the heart of the lord's keep, she knew she was close to what she wanted. Murdering the lord would prove her power. She wanted his blood this day, needed to see it shining on her axe blade, dripping at her feet.

Through corridors lined with tapestries and low-burning torches, she hunted. Servants' quarters lined the hall preceding a grand door. She reached for the handle, clamped her fingers over it, and made ready to pull it open.

"Althyn?" Her uncle's frightened voice interrupted her. "Dear one, let's flee. Let's go back to the ship. What you're doing..."

She shook her head at him and dragged the great door wide.

Chapter Fifteen
A Father's Revenge

LORD SALAK LAY in his bedchamber, the curtains partially drawn to reveal his prone form. He looked weak and vulnerable. Althyn stepped up to the foot of the bed and glared down at his shadowed shape. The rage she felt, the burning need to kill this man, made little sense to her. She took down the axe and readied it in her hands. A series of visions swept over her in which Salak leered over her or held up pouches of gold.

"I don't know you," she whispered. "Why do I feel like I do?"

The axe became heavier. Her father's voice drifted in her thoughts. "*Kill him, daughter. Kill that foul pig, and take everything he owns.*"

She shuffled to the side of the bed now, her body shrouded by the curtains. The axe lifted.

Anthis squeaked.

The blade fell, cleaving the sleeping man's head free from his body.

For the longest time, Althyn stood there staring at the black pool of liquid darkening the fine sheets. She smelled the scent of fresh death. Her body shivered. Her mind turned. Somewhere far away, she thought she heard her father cackling with glee.

Anthis tugged on her sleeve, but she didn't want to leave just yet. She wanted to watch the lord's body bleed. She wanted to reach out and draw her fingers through the mess she had made, maybe touch them to her lips, taste his soul.

"Althyn."

She faced her uncle.

"By the three sisters, you are your father's daughter and it breaks my cold heart to see it. Please, let's go. If we're caught—"

"No one can stop me." She pressed her lips together, sure of her words.

He drew his hand away and wrung it with the other one. "All right. All right, my Captain. We take the gold. We steal as much as we can carry."

She nodded. With a satisfied huff, she wiped the axe across the coverlet and shouldered the possessed tool. Together, they plundered the lord's bedchamber, taking any jewelry they found, weighing themselves down with trinkets and gold.

"Just how do you propose we leave the keep?" Anthis asked when they approached the door. Sunlight already filtered through the paned glass at the rear of the room. The keep would be teeming with servants and life. People would be going about their daily chores.

"We walk out."

He swallowed and shook his head, but as usual, he did not argue. She had the same power over him as her father had. She led the way out, and he obediently followed.

They made it as far as the stables before guards took notice. Shouts rang out. The men gave chase. Anthis darted away toward the open gate of the keep, but Althyn turned to face her enemies.

"Run!" her uncle screamed.

She waved a hand at him, dismissing his cowardice.

Humming, she summoned the winds, the water in the air, the rain impregnating the clouds high above. Thunder crackled. Holding one hand up at the men who approached, she willed a ray of ice to ensconce them, to stop them and freeze them in death. The element, *her* element obeyed.

Her targets dispatched and useless now against her, she laughed. Two men from the stable peered from behind the hitching post at her. A woman toting a basket covered her mouth with one hand.

Althyn laughed louder and went on her way, leaving behind the keep and its dead lord. She wanted more of this havoc, more chaos and more gold. Tapping one of her mate's stolen daggers, she realized she wanted more of him, too. But he would not find her where she went now. He could not possibly keep up, even though he'd managed to make pace with her when they had mated.

Uncle and niece traveled through the village, the docks, and made their way to the ship awaiting them. Lainious stood at the bow looking pensive and lost. "Mistress!" he shouted and flailed one arm in greeting.

Althyn crossed the plank and went to stand beside her servant.

"The crew abandoned us?" Anthis called, looking round with another bout of panic on his face. The wind picked up, trailing his greasy hair about his face in snakelike tendrils.

"I don't need them," Althyn replied. She stared up at Lainious. "Go and hoist the sails."

He nodded and left her side to do as he was told. She spied on her servant, thinking his attempt to please her before she had left to free her uncle meant nothing. He was weak, inexperienced, and subservient. She stared at his back, at the places the scars had been that she had erased. The heat surging through her veins was not the same as when she had taken Tolston. She glanced over her shoulder, up the rows of docks and past the milling crowds. There was no denying that she hoped her mate had given chase, but no one followed. No high guard stood in the distance with a vengeful glare on his handsome face.

When Lainious returned, the sails high, she ordered him to untie the ship and pull the anchor. Afterward, Althyn sang. Her voice lingered in the growing breeze, drawing the winds, drawing clouds and more threatening thunder. People hurried through their chores and took cover. The ship drifted away from Port Truias, and Althyn kept watch on the bow until the land became a distant mottle of shapes on the horizon.

"Where is the Othian Church?" she asked her slave. "I would go there now."

Lainious cleared his throat, his eyes cast down at his sandaled feet. "The nearest temple is to the east, mistress, on the island of Nemba. You have tired of me, mistress?"

"No." She traced his forearm with a tentative finger. "I will find this Assantra and take the treasures of the place that enslaved you."

"Please," he began, his voice softer than before, "let us sail anywhere but there. I am not worthy of your vengeance upon my past."

She snorted. "I don't do it for you, slave. Make no mistake of that." She pulled the axe free from her back, as well as the long sword, and handed them to him. "Take these and hang them on the wall beside my bed. I will start a collection."

He took the axe, but immediately dropped it.

Althyn glared.

"I'm sorry, mistress. It burns me. Its touch causes me to hear a voice."

She waved a hand and turned her back on him. "Find a way to take it to my room. I have no time for trivial games."

The waves turned angry to either side of the ship. A path of smooth water made way for her, though. Althyn sang in time with the ship's rocking. Her mind calmed and she set her will to the east, hoping to find the Othian Church before nightfall.

"Althyn," Anthis began, rounding beside her.

"What is it?" she snapped.

"There seems to be a ship…following us."

As soon as her song ended, the wind slowed. Her heart picked up speed. "Really?"

Althyn and Anthis strode across the length of the ship to peer at the vessel far behind them. "Do you think it's from Truias?"

"It is," her uncle answered. "It flies Lord Salak's colors."

She gripped the railing and squinted, hoping to see some sign of Tolston. Already, she missed his gruff voice and the feel of his beard abrading her cheek. She hated herself for the uncomfortable longing. It reminded her of her mother, of weakness and submission.

She sang to the sea and sky, hurrying back to her place at the head of the ship. The wind tousled her blonde hair, causing it to fly in wild wisps about her face. Power surged through her blood, commanding the element, as was her birthright.

The ship giving chase neither gained nor lost pace. Althyn kept searching it out over her shoulder at every given chance. A tightness set in her chest. She hoped it was Tolston, needed it to be him, and more than that, she needed to defeat him.

"Mistress, the Nemba mainland," Lainious said, taking a place beside her. He pointed at the horizon, and through the mist, the mottled shape of hills and mountains emerged.

"There is a harbor where we can dock and perhaps hide from those who follow."

"Show me," she ordered, setting a shaking hand on his arm. At once, a shiver ran through her body. She held her breath and vowed not to look her servant in the eye. She needed a man this night, and she didn't want it to be him lest she feel the burden of the same attraction she suffered after Tolston. It maddened her the closer they came to the mainland, to think her mate gave chase. Her breathing hastened. Her senses heightened.

"Just there," Lainious said, pointing at a gathering of harsh stones that jutted from the waves. "Can you...can you steer clear of the rocks?"

"Of course I can," she snapped, and spared a moment to glower at him. His lips turned down in a small frown. She thought of the morning before when he had knelt to please her. Althyn swallowed and faced the path ahead, her emotions roiling.

"I'm sorry, mistress. I didn't mean to question your abilities. You continue to amaze me."

Her chest puffed with pride. *I amaze every man who sees me.* She smiled despite herself. "Remember your place," she snipped, and she tried to remember hers.

The ship turned unnaturally, wood creaking and sails whipping with urgency. The vessel dodged the perilous rocks and made berth in the shallows of a jungle-laden harbor. The beach, a thin line of pale sand, welcomed Althyn to its surface. She was tired from her song, from the day's journey, and the heated burden of a mate who desired her, who she had chosen and who, she knew, she would choose once more if he ventured close enough.

"You must keep watch while I sleep this night."

Lainious nodded. "I will wake you if the Truias ship finds us."

"If they do, I'll call the sea to drown it and its crew."

Her servant nodded, a flash of fear in his blue eyes before he left her. She watched him go to take his place at the rear of the ship. Once he vanished from sight, she looked over the mist-laden landscape before her. "A new land," she whispered. "New treasures, new wonders for me to possess."

Soon after, she paced to her cabin below deck and lay upon her bed, staring at the axe and sword upon the wall. "I will have more weapons," she said. "A collection to rival Tolston's." She listened to the ocean singing and the far off call of her relatives until she drifted into sleep.

Althyn dreamed of Sherak, that he hovered over her bed keeping watch. His cold hands tested her face time and again. In his own tongue, he asked her to return with him to the tides. She understood his pleas, but told him no each time he asked. "I'm not ready," she explained. "I might never be ready to return to the mer. I do not know them."

Gulls cried in the distance, waking her. Lainious lay across the foot of the bed, warming her feet, his snores soft and soothing. She nudged him with her toe.

He jumped up with a start. "I'm sorry, mistress," he offered. "Your uncle is standing watch. I couldn't keep my eyes open any longer." He shimmied off the bed to reach over its side. "I've made you another pair of sandals, and boots as well."

"Good." She pushed off the mattress and went to the mirror to brush out her hair. "You will dress me for this visit to the church. You will prepare me to conquer all that I come across."

"Yes, mistress," he said, and she heard a hint of hunger in his low voice.

Chapter Sixteen
Othian Temple

ALTHYN WATCHED LAINIOUS lower the boat. She elbowed her uncle and said once more, "I could have pushed the ship to the beach with the tide."

"You are impatient," Anthis mumbled, waving a hand at her. "If you did such a thing, the hull would be smashed on coral or rocks. Trust me in this."

She heaved an angry sigh through her nose. Above her, Lainious shimmied down the rope, his lithe body pleasing in the dimming evening light. Each muscle on his arms rippled. The curls of his hair swayed against his tan back. She noticed the absence of scars on his skin when he sat before her, unlaced the boat, and began to row. The ability to make him hers, to remove all marks of his past, gave her a surge of strength and invincibility.

In a methodic rhythm, he leaned forward and backward, the oars breaching the water's surface and leaving ripples in their wake. She stared at his progress, slightly distracted by him. The dizziness no longer settled over her. She decided that since she'd chosen a mate, the uncontrolled attraction she seemed to feel for other men must be wearing thin.

Sand scuttled underneath the little boat. Her uncle clambered out first, looking grim about the venture. She followed. Her new boots made soft sounds as Althyn strode across the thin strip of beach in the direction her servant indicated. Her uncle waited for her to move ahead before he followed, wringing his hands and muttering under his breath about the danger of what they set out to do. Last in line came Lainious, Althyn's sword and axe tied across his back. She glanced back at him every so often after they entered the jungle, and it irritated her when warmth spread through her body, defying her mind. He looked handsome with the weapons. They didn't weigh him down and, indeed, he seemed to be standing taller than ever before, as if he had some unknown hope in his heart.

"There's a village near here, along the coast," Lainious said.

She slowed her pace until he caught up to her. Side by side, they moved into the undergrowth. Palms and vines obscured her view, but as they neared the place Lainious pointed out, she heard the noises of people. The village they overlooked was nothing like Truias. Here people milled about at their chores, hanging fish to dry, tying nets and herding animals over small roads. Fishing boats, much smaller than her father's ship, lined the single dock.

"They look poor," she complained.

"Yes," Lainious replied, "they are. I was born in that village and chosen by the Assantra when she came to collect tithes and my father couldn't pay."

Her eyes narrowed. "Well, I care nothing for the village. Take me to the temple, to the place where I can find the Othian Dagger and more riches. That is what I desire."

Lainious nodded. "There is a stone path we must follow deep into the jungle." He pointed out which way they needed to go.

The little band of three hurried along in the darkness. Animals moved nearby. Birds sang and chirped to each other when the sun dipped behind the horizon. Far ahead in the shadows of the trees, Althyn made out the hazy glow of torchlight. The closer they came along the pale stone path, the brighter the lights glowed. Eventually, tall torches lined the walkway, which in turn, joined with two other walks into a wide road.

The Othian Temple glittered with candlelight and more torches. A building carved from the stone of the mountain behind it. Stairs twisted and turned in endless labyrinth patterns. The lilting voices of female singers drifted through the night air, giving Althyn pause. "Why do they sing?"

"It's the end of the evening mass in worship of Othia. The priestesses will retire now to their rooms." In the flickering firelight, Althyn saw a strange gleam in Lainious's eyes. It could have been melancholy, or maybe he was remembering what it was like to be within the temple, but she didn't care either way.

They carried along, passing benches and a series of altars laden with flowers and offerings. Coins with the shape of the sun stamped onto them glittered. Althyn wanted to stop and take it all up, but she knew if such treasures waited unattended outside, that far greater plunder lay ahead.

"Tell me about Othia. What is it? What sort of god do these priestesses worship?" Althyn asked when they passed beneath a series of arches.

"Othia is the sun god. His followers pray to him at dawn, midday, and sunset." Lainious adjusted the straps on his shoulder, redistributing the weight of Althyn's weapons. "The Assantra believes he speaks through her."

Althyn thought on his words. It became clear to her that they had only breached an outer series of buildings. Lainious pointed at a narrow set of stairs, and they started their ascent.

"Does he?" she asked much later.

Lainious frowned when she halted and faced him.

"Does the god speak through the Assantra?"

He averted his eyes. "Yes, mistress. He does."

She nodded and went on. *If a god speaks to this woman and I kill her, then no one can stop me,* she thought. *Not even a god.*

Silent until now, Anthis began to mutter under his breath. Althyn stopped, losing patience with him. "Stay here and keep watch for my return."

He ran his fingers through his greasy hair and nodded. "As you wish, my dear. I think this temple is far out of my league."

"But not mine." She flashed a grin at him.

He swallowed and shuffled his feet. "You killed the Lord of Truias. Even your father was not capable of that...as much as he wanted to." When he looked her in the eye, she knew he was in awe of her. This made her proud.

"Stay here, Uncle. I will bring back a treasure for you."

He nodded, flattening his back against a wall. "I'll be here."

Althyn turned her back on him and hurried up the stairs, anxious now to find what she sought. The voices from earlier no longer echoed in the silence. She reached back and found Lainious's hand when the darkness surrounded them.

"Are you frightened?" he asked.

She snorted out a sudden laugh. "Frightened? Of what?"

He squeezed her hand. "Of the dark."

"I fear nothing." His closeness and the fact that they were now alone weighed on her senses. Heat settled in between them. Althyn started away, avoiding the euphoria that threatened. Lainious stayed at her side, his fingers knotted with hers.

"You make me believe I should fear nothing, too." Their footsteps echoed when they came to the end of the stairwell. Before them, a long corridor lit with small fire lamps spanned far into the temple's heart.

"You should always fear me," Althyn warned, "always."

"Yes, mistress." His voice echoed a sad sort of disappointment. She couldn't understand why. "I will take you through the servants' rooms where I used to live when the church owned me. There are secret passages that lead to the Assantra's bedchambers."

"Will you know this Assantra?"

"Assantra Izbeal is the sister of Assantra Elthia, who your father killed the day he stole me."

"I wonder, can you tell me how my father managed such a thing? My uncle just said my father couldn't kill the Lord of Truias and this temple is larger and more imposing than the hold."

"Elthia was on her way to another church in the north country when your father and his followers overtook the caravan. I found out later he didn't know who he had killed. It didn't give him pause to...murder women or children."

"No, it wouldn't. Which way now? It's late, and I want to be done with this before dawn."

Lainious pointed, and they moved through the corridors and secret ways until they came out in a honeycomb of rooms. Althyn liked the odds. It reminded her of when she had killed the Lord in Truias. There was not much challenge in taking someone's life in their bed. *Maybe this time there will be a fight.*

"Tell me about this Izbeal."

Lainious sucked in a breath, releasing it in a gust. "She did not care for me. It was Izbeal who burned the mark of undesirable into my skin."

"Undesirable?"

He ducked into a doorway and pulled Althyn with him. "Yes, mistress. So that I could not give the Assantra children, not that I had any hope of doing so."

She snorted. "Foolish woman. The only thing undesirable about you is your subservience."

His steps faltered.

Shadows clouded the hallway before them, and torchlight spilled into the darkness. Women's voices, low and gentle, hung in the air. "...this way, Sister Alise, not to the quarters. She'll lock us in the lowers again if she catches us."

Althyn drew a dagger from her belt and waited.

Two young women came into the passage. They slapped their hands over their mouths, eyes wide at having been discovered. One gasped in a muffled way and pointed behind Althyn at Lainious.

Impatient, Althyn threw her blade at the other girl, striking her in the chest. Her victim tumbled backward in a heap of pale temple robes.

The second girl shrieked and bolted back the way she'd come.

"Did you know them?" Althyn asked.

Lainious knelt beside the fallen young woman. "Not this one, but the other is the Assantra's daughter. She knows me."

"Good." She twisted her fingers through his hair. "Fetch my dagger for me. I'll not have a lost weapon."

He grimaced and wrenched the blade free of the body. After he wiped it across the woman's robes, he offered it back to Althyn. "As you wish."

"Shall we follow her?"

He nodded, his mouth set.

Together, they sprinted along the hall, side by side, their gait well matched. She hadn't thought he would be able to keep up with her. Bypassing arches draped with fabric, Lainious finally stopped. Women's voices broke into shouts and cries of horror far behind them. Her servant grabbed her arm and pulled her into the darkness. His eyes were narrowed as he drew his face to hers and pressed a lusty kiss to her lips. Althyn tensed.

Lainious kissed her with more fervor, pushing his tongue into her mouth. She held her breath and pulled away. "What are you doing?"

"Kissing you. You said the only thing—"

"I know what I said." She snarled at him. 'It didn't mean that I wanted, that you should..." She groaned, unsure of what to say next. "The dagger. Where is the dagger? You forget why I came to this place."

He backed away. "The Othian Dagger?"

"Yes. Enough of this foolishness between us. I've come here to kill the Assantra and take the dagger and whatever other relics I find. I will do what my father couldn't."

He sighed and ran his fingers through his dark hair. "The Othian Dagger is a powerful symbol, and a weapon that bears the magic of the god. Rumor has it that if someone other than a priestess touches it, her skin will burn as if the god touched her himself."

Althyn smiled. "Is it so? Have you touched it?"

"No, never."

"Where is it? Do they keep it in a shrine?'

"The Assantra wears it on her belt." He chewed at his cheek and looked away from Althyn. "I'm sorry I kissed you. I won't do so again unless you ask."

She tried to contain the laughter in her throat. "Oh, I will ask you. Make no mistake of that." She shot a sideways glance at him, but he turned away, hiding his expression.

"The Assantra's quarters are this way. It's likely she won't be there now, with the death of the girl."

"Then take me to her bedroom. I'll wait for her there."

"Yes, mistress. I should warn you, though. The Assantra is not helpless and weak like old Lord Salak was. Your uncle told me you killed him while he slept." This time, Lainious did look back, his eyes cold and serious. "You were lucky that night."

She glared at him. "Lucky?" She stuck her hands on her hips, indignation halting her. "I was not lucky. Luck had nothing to do with what happened."

He half smiled, but walked away rather than confront her. "You'll see. She knows magic. Not your kind of magic, for certain, but the Assantra has the magic of the sun god. She'll try to use it against you if you give her the chance."

Lainious had almost vanished at the end of the dark corridor he was leading her through before she gave in and followed. "What is her magic? How does it work? What will stop her?"

He ran his fingers along the carved stone walls, his face barely visible save the shaft of torchlight coming in from before them. As he traced each symbol, he spoke softly, warning her of what she was to face. "The god's magic is fire. She will have to concentrate to use it against you, and that takes time and energy. I think...since you like a good fight so much, that the Assantra will be a challenge."

"I will smite her as my father did the woman who kept you as her slave." She puffed out her chest and smiled.

"You will, I hope. The Othian Church has all but starved the people of this island." Lainious stopped, searched, and press his fingers into a slot on the wall. A stone shifted, grating against another, and soon a secret passage was revealed. "Although I make no assumptions that you are any kinder that Izbeal, sometimes one evil is better than another."

His words confused her, but she followed him into the pitch darkness, feeling her way forth until she touched his back and the shape of her father's axe strapped there. He had wrapped the weapon in linens to keep it from making contact with his skin. It affected him as it did her, only she knew why and how to deal with her father's soul.

"This way," he whispered. "We are nearly there."

Candlelight flickered behind the thick curtains they came to. Lainious paused. Both listened for any sign of someone in the chamber on the other side. "I think it's safe," he said.

Althyn pushed past him, slipping through the curtains and into a room she could not have imagined in all her fantasies. Everywhere her eyes sought, a treasure awaited. Fine silken pillows decorated a bed fit for a queen. Furs had been sewn into a massive blanket to keep the sleeper warm on the cold nights spent in the cavern-like temple. Oil paintings decorated one wall. The others were dressed with ornate tapestries dedicated to the sun god. Statuettes adorned a grand gilt table by the door. "Such riches."

"All taken from the people as tithes, willingly or unwillingly, at the tip of a blade or in lieu of taking children into slavery." Lainious stood by the curtains, stoic and sad. "I have slept in this room. Served the women who frequented here. Not all are cruel, but all serve the temple with the same zeal. They all steal lives in their calling to be one with Othia."

She walked around the room, taking in each detail, each gross display of wealth, and all Althyn could think was that she wanted it for herself. That she would make this room and all its possessions, the temple, the very people that worshipped here, her own.

Chapter Seventeen
Assantra

THE DOUBLE DOORS to the Assantra's chamber were closed. Althyn sat at the foot of the bed, her father's axe at one side, and her sword set across her lap. The lengthy weapon had yet to prove itself in a battle, but she longed to use it. Lainious went back through the passage to check on her uncle at her bidding. At first, he argued, but when she tapped the axe blade and narrowed her eyes at him, he finally left her alone with her thoughts.

Outside in the hall, she heard women's voices in passing, and the name of her servant mentioned several times. It was clear they thought he had killed the woman. *They will soon know the truth.*

When the doors to the chamber opened, and a woman strode in dressed in pale robes and gold slippers, her silver hair piled high on her head, Althyn grinned even wider. This was the woman who Lainious had feared? "You're nothing but an old hag," she said under her breath.

The Assantra froze, her eyes flickering with shock. "What is the meaning of this? Who are you?" Her hand lowered to the dagger in her belt, the only weapon, Althyn noticed, that the older woman had on her person.

"I've come to dethrone you." She pushed up from the bed and gripped the long sword with both hands. "And to take from you this temple and all its followers. Your riches will be my riches. Your people will bow to me."

The woman hissed. "Ridiculous. Do you know who you speak to? Do you know who I am?"

"Yes... A ghost that doesn't know it's dead yet." She raised the sword as high as she could, and its tip nearly touched the ceiling. "Now come, let me show you your god. You will meet him this night."

The little dagger came free of its sheath at the Assantra's waist and glittered in the light cast from the hearth. It looked insignificant, small, powerless. But when it began to glow a fiery orange, Althyn knew she wanted it. She swung the gigantic sword at the woman, charging forth.

The Assantra tumbled to the floor, dodging Althyn's attack. "What kind of woman are you?" she shrieked. "This is my chamber. Get out! Guards!"

"No one can stop me," Althyn said, more to herself than her opponent. "This place is *mine*."

"I don't even know who you are!" The woman scrambled across the rug.

Althyn swung. "Everyone will know my name soon enough."

The Othian Dagger flew through the air in a sad effort to stop her. It sliced through the sleeve of Althyn's dress before it hit an oil painting, which immediately caught fire.

"Is that all you can do?"

The woman backed to the bed, pushing herself away with her feet. "Guards!" she screamed again, her voice hoarse. "Guards! Help me!"

The sound of bootsteps pounded in the hall. At that moment, Althyn realized she hadn't planned on interference. She looked over her shoulder, hesitating.

Heat burst across her fingers. She screeched and let go of the sword. "You tried to burn me!" She faced the Assantra and reached for her father's axe. Its evil soul numbed the pain she had felt moments before. She felt him in there, gleeful at what his daughter was about to do and...proud. She swung, bringing back memories of the horrible night her parents had died. She sliced and chopped and hacked again and again until there was nothing left that could burn her again.

The guards came, but halted when they found Althyn standing by the bed, blood spattered and the Othian Dagger in her fist. "I am your Assantra now. Go and tell them. Tell them all that Nemba belongs to Althyn Laethwyn!"

The guards' faces were a blur to her, mostly women, with a few men scattered within. One came forward, his brown eyes dark and sad. "What have you done?" he accused over and over. He wore little but a loincloth to cover his crotch. His weapon was a rusted spear that he carried halfheartedly. Locks of unruly, light brown hair framed his plain face. "Izbeal," he stammered, and turned his face to retch.

"Out!" Althyn shrieked. "Go and tell them what I have said!"

Slowly, the followers obeyed, backing away from the horrible scene and watching her with fear.

Lainious and Anthis burst through the curtain to join her sides. "You've done it," her uncle muttered. Lainious let out a small, startled breath.

"I have," she said. "I've taken this place. It's mine now."

The guard who had lost his stomach sat up and stared at her. "You've murdered a great woman, the voice of a god. That's all you've done."

"So what if one god is silenced? A god of slaves, I am told. Worship me, instead." She flicked her hair from her shoulder and sauntered toward the guard. "What were you to this...Assantra that you should care about her death?"

"A priest of Othia," he said, standing up to face her. He was only a little taller than she, and Althyn stood straight to glare into his eyes.

"A priest of lies. Bow down to me now or I will punish you for your disloyalty." She pointed at the bloodstained floor.

"I will never bow to you. You're nothing more than a tyrant."

She smirked and took a step closer. "Be careful what you say to me, Priest." Althyn reached out and grabbed a fistful of his hair. "What is your name?"

"H-Harold Nathgow."

She laughed. "You're nothing but a lowly reptile to be squashed, a hideous mutation of cowardice thinking it has a moment of courage. I curse you." She tugged his hair, drawing him to her. He stumbled and fell to his knees. Her body rushed with heat and power, the dangerous magic of her ancestors all mixed and jumbled between elvish and mermish ends. "Scales," she whispered, imagining his skin covered with such. "And a tail to flick at the sun each time it rises. To curse your god with what you have become."

He whined out a pained groan. His face contorted. The lavender-gray mist that so easily surrounded her when she gazed into the eyes of a man appeared from the very air. As she had thought them into being, green reptilian scales burst from the unfortunate priest's flesh. They covered his arms, his legs. A tail burst from his backside, curling and slapping at the wall behind him as it grew. It was not a beautiful transformation, not something she liked to behold. But it served its purpose.

Althyn shoved him away from her. "Go from this temple, you monster!" she shouted. "Go and let all who see you know what I am capable of. This is what happens to those who do not swear loyalty to me!" She released him, and he cowered, staring down at his hands in horror. The cursed man crawled away, weaponless, changed forever by what she had done. Lainious stepped before her, his eyes wide.

"Did you see what I did?" she said in a quiet voice.

"I did, mistress. Everyone saw."

"Clean up this mess," she said, and bypassed him, axe in hand, to see what other treasures awaited her in her new home.

As she walked the halls of the temple, its followers fled, some abandoning their home in panic, a few remaining behind to watch their new leader. She passed through gilded corridors and columns carved of fine, white marble until she reached a high dais. There, Althyn overlooked the little village built upon the crags and beach below. It belonged to her now, all of it, the people, the homes, everything. She stared at the ocean beyond, with the bright white moon reflecting off its waves. Out there, her destiny awaited, but for now, she could stand here and be in control of an entire island. She could have slaves to care for her, to feed her and pamper her.

A man's voice interrupted her thoughts of victory and possession. "Well, looks like I've found you again, pretty one."

His rough hand covered her mouth before she could utter a sound. "What have you done? Killed a lord and now come to beg forgiveness from Othia?" He crushed his hardness into her backside and breathed heavy into her ear. "Who will stop you? Who can stop something like you? I swear, you are the tide coming in during a violent storm. Overtaking all that you touch. Drowning it. Killing it with your fierce beauty." Tolston sucked her earlobe past his lips and nibbled at her.

Althyn shivered. The tempestuous mist surrounded them, enveloping her in a heady, needful wave of lust. Her mate had found her. He had come to claim her once more. And though she was dotted with the blood of her victim, she wanted him to take her here.

He ground himself against her body and lowered his hand from her lips to paw at her breasts. Soon her dress slipped down and away. The wind carried a sorrowful tune to her elvin ears from the sea. But Althyn didn't want to listen to its plea. She arched her body and let her mate press her against the cold stone wall. She begged for more when he pushed himself into her and claimed her body as he had done time and again in his room. Even as she cried out in ecstasy when he slipped his fingers into her folds and touched her as she wanted to be touched, she hated him. She loathed him and this temporal power he had over her instincts.

His length slammed inside her body, making her quiver and groan. He came in a burst of tension and muscles, driving her down to the cold tiles on the floor. The wind picked up and cooled their sweat-beaded bodies. Tolston took her wrists in one hand and forced them over her head, pinning her as she had done to him on their last meeting. When he drew a cold blade and set it at her neck, she smiled at him. "You like this game, don't you?"

He laughed down at her. "Game? Someone must stop you, temptress. There is a high price on your head now." He kissed her lower lip, his beard scratching her already sore chin.

When his mouth raised, she said, "I have gold to pay such a price if that's all you desire. Icy coins in your palm and bouncing in your purse. Is that all you want? Metal to warm your bed at night?"

"When I want something, I take it. Like I've taken you."

"I take what I want, as well."

"Mm. What a match we make then." He nipped at her mouth, and then let his blade fall beside her. "In a little while, I'm going to take you again. I'm going to keep at it until you scream my name and swear I'm the only one for you. And then, I'm going to leave you wanting."

She curled her hands into his hair and stared into his eyes. "What could I want here in this place? I have all I could ever want."

"No." He panted, his grin wicked. "A creature like you always wants. You will want more in time. Maybe not now, not in the morning. But in a few days' time, you will want more. There will never be enough gold for you." He kissed her neck, his teeth grating into her soft skin. "You will want more swords, more axes, more dresses...maybe even a corset."

She ran her nails down his back, abrading his skin through his tunic. "Say my name. Don't call me pretty one. My name. I want to hear it from your lips."

He pushed his hand between their bodies until his fingers slipped into her cleft. Deeper he went, thrumming and teasing until she squirmed. "Say it," she said again, her voice quivering like her body.

"Althyn." He devoured her mouth and said her name again and again between his painful kisses.

Chapter Eighteen
Othian Dagger

DAWN SPILLED IN through the massive chamber's window, the curtains drawn to let in the great light of Othia. Althyn opened her eyes and stared at the brilliance, unmoved by its beauty. Tolston's arm was curved over her waist. His hot breaths fell against her bare shoulder as he slept. This was not as it had been with her mother and father. They had stopped sleeping in the same bed when she was a small child, if her father even slept at all when he was on the island. She looked down at Tolston's fingers, which rested on her abdomen. They were blocky and strong, fingers used to causing harm.

Something moved in the corner of the room. She squinted to avoid the light and saw Lainious sitting in the shadows, sewing. "Good morning, mistress," he said. "Your uncle has gone to the store rooms to take stock of the temple's holdings."

She slipped out of her lover's hold and pulled a robe over her nakedness. She knew Lainious had left the garment at the foot of the bed for her. "That is well and good." Althyn went to the table by the window and stared at herself in the looking glass there. It was an ornately framed mirror, more beautiful than the one on her ship. Her lips and chin were pink from Tolston's abrasive affections. Bruise-like marks from his lips ran down each side of her neck, and her hair was knotted. She sat down and frowned, reaching for a brush.

"Let me," Lainious said, and stood from his chore to come and comb out the tangles in her hair. In a low voice he asked, "What are you doing, mistress?"

She watched him work through the mats, gently righting what had gone wrong in the night. "He is not worthy of you. Not this one."

"And you are?"

Lainious looked at her through the mirror, his reflection piercing. "I didn't say that. I only want to warn you about what kind of man Tolston is."

"He's like my father." She sucked her lower lip into her mouth and stared at Tolston in the looking glass, his naked rear showing from the covers. "Why should I not choose such a man?"

"Because you understand what your father was and why your mother shouldn't have chosen him."

"I think she had little choice in the matter. Neither did I. The instinct floods my mind. I can hardly think. And now that's it's done..." She frowned. "Yes, it's done. No turning it back. No changing my choice."

Lainious continued to work in silence until he had braided her hair and tied it neatly. "I will follow your will, whatever that may be. But I think he is wrong for you. I think you will regret him."

Tolston mumbled and sat up, reaching his arms high in the air. He yawned. "Get that slave of yours out of here," he slurred. "Only one cock in the henhouse. Lest you want a fight, pretty one."

Althyn was not amused. "If you want to pick a fight, pick one with me."

He snorted at her and rolled out of the bed. His hair stuck up at the back of his head. He wiped his eyes. She admired his naked body and all the hair that covered him, his legs, arms, and chest. He reminded her of a wild thing that could never be tamed. "If it's a fight you want, woman, I'll give you one." He came up behind her and set his hands on her shoulders while Lainious went to gather clothes for her.

Her servant set a gown on the table before her. "You should address the congregation, those that stayed behind, mistress. They have gathered in the temple hall as they usually do at daybreak."

Tolston laughed. "You think to usurp the power of the church, woman?"

"I have already done so." She leaned her face to one side so that his arm touched her cheek. The hair there felt warm and comforting. She breathed in his scent, mesmerized by the flavor of his skin. Her eyes slipped shut, and she imagined herself climbing back into that ornate bed with him to waste away the morning as they had done most of the night.

"I'll be taking you back to Truias this afternoon, back to the cells or to my room, whichever you prefer."

She snorted out a quick laugh. "You will do no such thing."

"Your father was a criminal. You're a criminal."

"I hardly think you are much better, hiding behind that guard title. Your brother told me what kind of a man you are."

"Hmph. He talks too much when he should be getting to business."

She looked into the mirror at Tolston's face reflected there. "Do you know whose bed you slept in this morning?"

"Yours," he said, his eyes flickering over her chest.

"It was the former Assantra's bed."

He frowned at her. "And why is she a former Assantra?"

She shrugged. "Because before I dragged you by the beard into this chamber and had my way with you, I killed her in this very room. That's why there is no rug on the floor by the bed, and why the tiles still smell of fresh pine oil soap."

"Rather than the spilled blood of a sorceress?" He didn't smile, or look the least bit impressed or amused. "It's a very dangerous thing you've done."

She pushed up from the seat and spun to face him. "Ah, but the point is, I have done it. Nothing and no one can stop me. When I want something, I take it."

"Really?" He took hold of her thick braid and tugged her to one side. "Because I don't think you have any concept of the wrath the Othians will bestow on you for what you've done. The Sun God is a vengeful deity, capable of smiting those who defy his will."

She shrugged and forced a smile. His hand was tight about her hair, and it hurt. It excited her too. "I have not felt the heat of his wrath."

"You will. In time. He will do so at the right moment and make an example of you."

"I believe there are no gods except those that your kind make up to gather followers and riches. That's all this place is. A temple of lies."

"Lies." He huffed and pulled away, his fist still tight about her hair. She followed unwillingly, trying her best to look as though she were in control. He shoved her onto the bed. "By all means, pretty one, get dressed and address the followers of the god you blaspheme. I want to see the sun's light shine on your skin when you speak in the Assantra's place."

"The sun cannot hurt me. It never has."

"There's a first time for all things." He gripped her face in his other hand and held her still while he leaned forth to plunder her mouth. The kiss was violent, hard, and forced. She heard Lainious leave the room, his footfalls quick. After the door shut, Tolston shoved Althyn away and pulled on his clothes, which had been strewn across the foot of the bed. He laced up his trousers and forced his feet into his boots. "I'll have to hurry to get a good seat. I wonder...will your skin smell as sweet when it's singed by the light of Othia?"

She sighed and glared at him. Althyn went to the table to gather up her dress. She stepped into the garment and tied the sides as best she could without the help of a servant. "You watch. No god will dare to touch me. Gods don't exist. They forsook this world long before I was brought into it."

He raked his fingers through his hair, and clenched his jaw, the muscle in his cheek tensing beneath his beard. Then, Tolston stomped out, leaving the doors wide. She heard a muffled cry of pain, a man's voice. Soon after, Lainious came into her chamber, holding his left eye.

"He dared to hit you?" She stiffened, angry that he would touch her property.

He nodded, his lips pursed tight.

"Fix this dress," she ordered, and waved a hand at her servant. "I *will* go to the temple hall now."

"Yes, Althyn." He went to her side and tightened up the poorly laced sides of her dress. With his help, she put on her boots, and he gestured to the Othian Dagger that lay on the table. "Have you touched it yet?" he asked.

She reached for the weapon, confident in herself, and that it would not affect her. Her fair fingers closed over the piece, a solid casting from the tip of the sharp blade to the end of its hands. The sun shape above the grip shimmered. For a moment she felt a sizzle of energy, the echo of a man's voice, then nothing. It was as any other dagger that had no charm upon it. "All the followers of Othia are human?"

"Yes, mistress. No elves. None of the lesser races like the trolls and dwarves."

She nodded to herself. "Of course not. Why should such beings worship Othia?" She thought this very fact explained her immunity to what they all feared. Othia was worshipped by humans, and although her mother had appeared human when she died, she never truly was that.

"It is more simply that they are not allowed into the temple. The Assantras inspect every potential initiate. If such impurities of the blood as mixed races appear, they are turned out or executed."

She took the blade and held it up, satisfied. "Let me go and speak to my new followers. See how they will fear me when I hold up this silly blade."

"All who see you will fear you in time, Althyn." Lainious's voice held a tone of melancholy, as well as pride.

He followed a step behind her as she left the chamber and went along the passage. Even then she could hear the sounds of many voices gathered in song. They were the voices of women, mostly, sweet and peaceful, like her mother used to sound when she sang to the sea.

"You have done a great thing, mistress."

She stopped and waited for him to halt at her side. "What great thing?"

"You have stopped the evil on this island, rid the people of something that would, in time, have killed them all with its greed."

She fingered her dress with her free hand, thinking what his life before her must have been like. "They stole you from your parents. Raised you here to do as they wished. Are there many like you?"

"Hundreds of children."

She fisted the fabric of her skirt. "At least I knew my mother. You had no knowledge of yours?"

"None." He was looking Althyn in the eyes, something he rarely did. "Do you know how much good you could do here?"

She cleared her throat, put off by his words. "Good." She shook her head. "What good can evil do? You knew my father. You have seen what I've done since leaving my mother's cottage. I am not good. Not good in any way. The last of any kindness and goodness I may have had died on that island with my mother."

He reached for her and ran a finger along the back of her hand, ever so close to the dagger. She saw his fear of the weapon, his doubt. But he believed in her, and it was an empowering truth. He thought she had murdered the Assantra for some greater good. He saw her as something powerful, wonderful. "Lainious, what am I to you?"

"I love you, mistress. Like a man loves water when he has not drank for days."

"Love?" She let go of her dress and set her palm against his face. "How can you possibly love me?"

"How could I not?" He placed his hand over hers. His blue eyes reminded her of the clear sea at dawn when she used to stare at it as a child and wonder what lay across it. "You have done things that are not possible, destroyed every boundary set before you. You have erased my past and given me a future. I will love you for the rest of my days."

"What is love, really? A trick of nature to set two beasts to mating. That's all I see in it. I despise love. I shun it. It makes one weak to passions that should be resisted."

"You do not love Tolston."

"Of course not," she snapped. "How could I possibly? He's vulgar and cruel."

"Yet you give yourself to him."

She curled her upper lip. "You would not take me when I wanted it so." She took her hand away from his face and stomped away. "Blame yourself for his presence here, if you must. I have no more control of the instincts bred into me than my mother and father did."

She hurried away, disliking the truth in her words. If she were to leave this island, would Tolston follow? Would he return to her every month to celebrate their first union as her father had with her mother? Would her end be as cold and cruel as her mother's had been, and at the hands of the mate she had chosen? These questions puzzled her as she entered the temple and wound her way through a series of statues to the stage where the former Assantra must have delivered speeches and lies to the people sitting on the benches below.

All the beautiful voices went silent. She took her place at a gilded podium and held the dagger high above her head. Althyn's eyes sought through the watchers until she found the one she wanted to see. Tolston had indeed taken his place in the front row, his expression aloof and cold. His arms were crossed over his chest, and she thought he looked handsome there in the light shining down from the great glass window at her back.

"Behold," she began, sending her voice out across the listeners. "I hold the dagger of Othia, of your false god, and it has not destroyed me. No one can destroy me or take what I have claimed as my own."

Whispers broke out and soon fell silent.

"This temple, this island, all of you, belong to me now. All priestesses and priests that remain in this temple must swear allegiance to me by nightfall, or leave this place forever." She felt the heat of the sun shining at her back, warming her, although the temple was chilly inside, cave-like. The dagger's touch made her skin crawl at that moment.

Tolston stood, his eyes widening.

Althyn held the small blade tighter, defiant and determined. Some sort of change was trying to overtake her, be it the will of the god that had been worshipped here or another kind of magic she could not understand. She felt its heated touch, its urgency to meld with her mind. And she resisted.

Chapter Nineteen
Scaled Priest

ALTHYN DIDN'T LIKE the new sizzle of power that swept through her body, or the way all the onlookers stared up at her in awe. They didn't watch her with the usual fascination brought on by what she was. It was as if some light exuded from her, some heavenly glow that she had no control over. She opened her mouth once more to address the gathered followers, but the words that slipped from her mouth were not her own. "Every child taken from the village by the sea will be returned to its family this day. There will be no more slaves stolen in the name of the god, and no more unwilling servants in this temple."

Her mouth snapped shut. She tried to set the dagger in her belt, but no matter how she willed her hand to do her bidding, her fingers remained curled around the blade's handle. Frustrated, she waved her other hand at the people below and marched out. This was not what she had wanted. Althyn was greedy for riches, shiny baubles to ponder and rich trinkets to occupy her time. She wanted a wall of weapons like Tolston had, and many more servants like Lainious to wait on her and do as she wished.

In the hall to the bed chamber, Lainious was waiting for her, his blue eyes wide and mystified. "What you have done this day... It is a good thing, a great good that will be remembered always."

She scowled at him, but didn't want to admit she had no say in the matter. He might think her weak. As it was, he was impressed by the deed. Impressing him couldn't hurt. She hurried into the room and was able to toss the charmed blade onto the dressing table, releasing it and its strange passions at last. Glaring at it, she made a small vow not to touch the dagger directly again. Who knew what it might make her do? And why had it not done so to the prior priestesses?

She paced by the window, pondering the mystery of the blade. Certainly, her father's axe was magicked, but not like the dagger. She felt no soul within that little piece of metal. "It must channel energy," she said aloud. "But I will not touch it again. Oh no."

The door shut abruptly. She heard the distinct sound of the metal bar dropping into place. Without turning, she knew it must be Tolston come to taunt her with his lust. Her heart hammered in her chest. She sucked in a deep breath and smiled. "You want more of what I've given you?"

The gravelly voice that responded made her frown. "You've given me enough, sorceress."

Althyn spun around and found the banished priest from the day before. He was hideous now, a horrible melding of reptile and human flesh. His long, green tail swished and slapped, hitting the bed leg and then the stand by the dressing table. He held a walking stick, hardly a weapon at all, against her.

"You." She *tsk*ed. "I sent you away, fool. Get out of this temple. It's mine!"

He stepped toward her, hands gripping the stick in tight fists. His dark eyes were angry, his mouth clenched, and his teeth showing.

"Get out!" she shrieked, angry that he would dare to disobey her.

"It is you who must leave." Another step. Another. His tail crashed into the bed's post, shaking the wood and leaving a dent. "What manner of evil are you? Cold and beautiful. Cruel and mesmerizing to look upon. You are not of this world."

She didn't like his insult. It touched too close on what she believed might be the truth. "I am what I am, you nasty, little lizard man. And you are two steps from death. Come at me if you dare. I'm in no mood to play games."

She stepped to the side, closer to the sword and axe, which Lainious had hung on the wall by the bedside. She supposed she didn't need them, that she could call upon the elements and freeze the priest, but injuring him, drawing his blood before she ended him, appealed to her.

His clawed hand moved ever so quickly, drawing a small throwing blade from the belt of his loincloth. He flicked his wrist and it was airborne, flying straight for her. She ran at him, forgetting the need of the sword. Her hands reached. She felt a slap of sharp pain in her shoulder. Heat followed. Wet heat. Her fingernails extended into talons. He grimaced when they collided and she scratched at his face, the only fully human part of him left. The scent of blood rent the air, his and hers mingling, coppery. He broke free, but not before she wrenched his stick from his hands.

Staggering, the lizard man wiped his scaled arms across his ruined cheek, blood streaking across his iridescent scales. He growled and reached for his belt, his hand finding purchase on another throwing knife. "You are like me now," he said with a sarcastic laugh. "Half human, half beast."

She glanced at her arms, covered with gold, birdlike scales, so much like her sister gryphon that it made her want to weep. Her back itched. Much longer fighting with him and she knew she would transform wholly. Althyn fixed the lizard man with a cold glare. "There is no part of me that's human." She charged him again, hungry for the taste of his blood, for the feel of flesh filling her mouth. The instinctual drive to kill him, to attack her prey, overwhelmed her. She had a fleeting thought that shifting her shape might be dangerous, a terrible way to lose herself to the creature she became. She slashed at his chest with her talons.

He screamed in agony, staggering backwards and away until he slammed into the wall.

Bloody lines formed across his skin between his nipples. Circlets of crimson grew and began to dribble down. They pattered on the floor as she panted. The cuts were not as deep as she would have liked. But he looked down and then back at her, his face reflecting defeat and disappointment.

"You are nothing to me," Althyn whispered. "Nothing, and no one will mourn your death. No one will know what became of you." She lunged.

He cowered and bumped his head on the axe handle. The weapon fell off the hanger and hit the floor at the lizard man's feet.

He moved out of her reach before she could sink her talons into his soft, thick flesh. Althyn squawked when her claws dug into the plastered wall, lodging there. The defeated man beneath her struggled to crawl away. She tugged and fought to free herself.

"You'll never rule this temple, not wholly," he said.

She managed to get her right hand out. Althyn half turned and screeched in surprise. He had hold of her father's axe. Worse, he was almost to the dressing table. He meant to steal the Othian Dagger! He meant to take what belonged to her. She tugged her talons free, showering the floor with bits of ruined plaster.

"Mistress!" Lainious shouted outside the door.

"Don't touch that!" She ran across the room and reached for the lizard man. His tail crashed into her. She teetered and fell clumsily onto the tiles. The priest snatched up the dagger, gave her a sly, sideways smirk, and ran for the window. She watched as he slipped the temple's most notorious relic into that thin belt that kept his loincloth on. With two swings of the stolen axe, the stained glass shattered and tinkled all across the floor.

The lizard man looked back at her, his face twisting into an evil visage of anger and hatred, an expression she knew so well. Her dead father's soul had done this, taken control of that simple minded priest and found a way to escape, at least to escape her.

She called to the wind that rushed into the bed chamber from the sea outside. It answered, but not as swiftly as she would have hoped. The priest leaped through the opening, scraping his malformed body on jagged pieces of glass. Then, he was gone through that escape into the outside world. "I'll get you," she vowed. And she knew, in time, she would do just that. No one defied her and got away with it. No one stole from her and should expect to live.

She raised herself up, her hands and arms gradually reshaping themselves. Althyn limped to the door, pulled up the bar and let her servant in. At once, his face showed his fear.

"Mistress, you're hurt." He reached for the blade buried in her shoulder and held it tightly. "Let me pull it free and staunch the bleeding. Who did this to you?"

"That priest. Harold something. The lizard. He has stolen my axe and the Othian Dagger. I want him found." She winced when Lainious slipped the blade from her flesh. He used his hand to put pressure on the wound, which bled profusely nonetheless.

"Sit down. Hold still until I can bandage this properly."

"Where is that useless mate of mine? He should be chasing after that thief. He should capture him and return my things to me." She let her servant guide her to the dressing table, and sat there while he struggled with one hand to find a piece of cloth to bind her wound. "You're being ridiculous," she finally told him. "Take your hand off of me. I'll sing it away."

He looked uncertain, but let go when she went to place her hand on the cut. She hummed under her breath and closed her eyes to concentrate. Torn flesh melded. Skin reattached and closed off the blood that wanted to escape. It made her lightheaded, but she lifted her palm when her song was done and nodded. "You see?"

"Thank Othia, you're all right."

"I'm fine now. Go and fetch my mate. Tell him I want that priest found and brought to me. Dead or near death."

Lainious looked down. "Tolston..."

"Yes, go and fetch him. Do as I say."

He shook his head. "It is midday. His ship has set sail."

A surge of rage ran through her in which she thought she could destroy anything and everything in her path. "He left me!" She stood up from the bed, and the dizziness that had settled over her from healing her wound kicked in again. Black splotches wavered in her field of vision. She reached for something to cleave to, to keep from fainting. As always, Lainious steadied her, and kept her upright.

"He can't leave me."

"He is a foul, disloyal man. Selfish and greedy. He has no need for only one woman in his life."

She ground her teeth and let her servant settle her on the bed. "I feel sick," she muttered. "Like I need to vomit."

"I'll fetch a wash pot."

She lay still, staring up at the fanciful fabric that covered the bedposts and obscured the ceiling. This was a safe place to be, a nest. The temple was hers. *That's what matters,* she reasoned. Not that her mate had abandoned her. "What need do I have of him?" she said aloud. "Brute that he was. He served no purpose other than to sate my body's lust."

Lainious returned to her side. Her servant washed the blood from her skin after removing her ruined dress. "Rest," he told her. "I will take care of everything for you." She closed her eyes and listened to him breathing above her as he cleansed her skin. Time slipped away. She felt pain working at her body, trying to take over and destroy her. She heard the clink of pieces of glass being cleaned up from the floor. The swish of a straw broom. The creak of the wooden shutter being pulled into place to cover the broken window and keep out the sea air.

She drifted in that thin world between waking and dreams, and she heard her cousin's voice, distant and sad, speaking into her mind. "*You have chosen a mate,*" he told her. "*And he was not what you should have wanted. You will suffer the same misery as your mother did now, caught between what your mate wants you to be and what you are. What you are is already an anomaly.*"

She tried to ignore the truth in his words. Tolston was just like her horrible father in so many ways. Maybe that was why she was drawn to him. Althyn's mind turned to the sea, to the feel of water against her skin and the freedom she had felt when she dipped beneath its surface and became what her mother truly was. Her body convulsed with strange shivers. As soon as the sick feeling that had come over her went away, she vowed she would get to her ship and move on. As safe as this haven felt, she needed to get away, needed to keep moving. *I should not stay in any one place as my mother did. I should move on. Find other wonders to make my own.*

"He's poisoned you, mistress. That damned priest tipped the blade. There's a line of the blackness reaching across your skin." Lainious set his hand on her forehead and it felt cool, so gentle. "I will make an antidote. But I must go to the seashore and find the plants I need. There are a few men left in this place that I know and trust. I will have them watch over you. A priestess, too, an initiate. She is young, but fierce, and she is also a storyweaver. I will have her stay at your side."

"Yes," she said, sounding weak. "Yes, you will look after me. My Lainious. My servant. You are so loyal. You must never leave me." She reached out and found his hand, tightening her grip to reassure herself that he would do as he said.

"Never, Althyn. I will always serve you."

Chapter Twenty
Storyweaver

"YOU ARE WITH child already." It was a cold, unfeeling voice devoid of emotion. "It is a shame."

Althyn turned her head to the side. The bed chamber was dimly lit by flickering tallow lamps. She made out the shadow of the being standing next to the bed. She squinted. "Who's there?"

He sighed and came ever closer until he seated himself beside her. "We have not been apart long enough for you to forget me."

She shivered. Her stomach lurched.

He placed his cold palm on her cheek. His skin smelled of seaweed, and his voice was familiar now. He rubbed her face with tenderness and leaned in so she could see him. "I followed your manservant to this place. I watched over you as he forced his potion into you. You are lucky he knows of such things."

"Sherak."

"Yes, cousin. It is only me, come to look after you. I daresay that uncle you love so much is useless. He's drunk himself unconscious while muttering his worries that you will die and he will have failed your mother." He made a small, sarcastic laugh before he went on, as if Anthis's state amused him. "Althyn, you are a wild thing given to impulse, much like your mother was. Think before you act. Your life is ever plotted by the decisions you make or do not make, as the case may be."

"My mother was not wild." She snorted at the thought, remembering the woman who had reared her on that empty island. She had been kind and gentle, teaching her the way of their sheltered world so that she might survive. Her mother used to sing to the sea and to Althyn, sweet songs that told no stories of being wild or making wrong choices...save one. She changed the subject, concerned over what he had said. "You said I was with child."

"Yes, you are, if only barely."

"How can you tell such a thing?"

"Your mate left. The attraction is binding only as long as you do not conceive. Once that has happened, he will leave, only to return when he feels the call of your body again. That may be a year, as the body takes months to recover from birth."

"No," she said, confused. "My father left and came back over and over. But he did leave us."

"Your mother knew a great many secrets about herbs and the ways of the body. I am sure she knew how to destroy any child that might have hooked itself into her human womb."

She thought back. Her mother had many little vials of dried up plants and roots by the hearth. She had seen her drink teas made from some of them, teas she would not share and would cringe at after sipping. Maybe it was true. "But why would she do such a thing?"

His fingers trailed to her chin, passed over her lips, and then he pulled his hand away. "You still desire your chosen mate, don't you?"

"Yes."

"You want to feel his body against yours; you crave his touch like a flower craves the light or the need for water. Sometimes this pain of loneliness is too much to bear. Perhaps your mother felt like this. She wanted him to return to her and had no need for another child. She had you, after all."

He leaned in even closer until his lips brushed her earlobe. "You have only to ask, and I will kill this mate of yours. The bond will be broken. I want nothing in return. You can be greater than what you've become, but you must learn to control your urges. I know they can be so strong, tempting enough to make you lose control. But you are better than this, Althyn. You don't understand what you are meant for." He sat up and ran his thumb over her lips. "Say the word, and I will do this small favor for you."

"You want something of me," she accused. Her mind turned over the revelation that a child could be growing inside her right now. A babe, helpless, its blood a mix of mermish, elf, and human. A little mess that would be even more confused than she. Althyn also imagined what it would be like if Tolston were dead. Sherak said strange things, but he knew the mermish side of her. Her eyes narrowed. Or maybe he wanted to use her for his own purposes. "You're trying to trick me."

"No. I admit my affection for you. I have no need to lie." His attention wavered, his eyes examining the room and then returning to her. "You will change your mind about the male you've chosen, or go the way of your mother in time. The mer are shape-shifters, cousin. We change like the tide when the wind wills it this way or that. Our moods make us love one moment and hate the next. Honesty is a fleeting thing among my kind, *our* kind, but my honesty has always been steadfast, just as I believe your need to wander will not wane."

She turned away from him. She did feel the need to wander, to discover, to find more forbidden treasures. Althyn saw the silhouette of the girl Lainious had promised. The skinny wench was asleep in the bedside chair, her head turned to the side while she snored. Some good she was. She figured he would have posted the men outside her room to offer her privacy.

"If you don't believe me, maybe you could test the theory. Ask that manservant of yours to make the potion I speak of. He will know such things. He knew how to counter the poison that priest gave you. A child losing potion is a small thing to make compared to that. Your mate will return soon after the child leaves your body. And you will be happy for a time."

She didn't want to think about such a thing. Instead, she focused on Sherak's cold eyes and the serious expression on his unusual face. Changing the subject, she said, "I don't want Tolston dead."

He nodded. "I understand. Perhaps not yet. Many mer grow weary of their landmates, when they make such a choice as you have done. Should that time come, I am only a song away from the sea. I will be ever listening for your voice, as I have waited for it all my life."

"If I want him dead, I will kill him myself. I have no need of your aid." She snarled at him, angry that he would think her weak and mindless. "I chose my path. I will always choose the way I go and the partner I bed. You will wait for me until the end of your days."

"Oh, but my dear one, you do not understand. Our kind mate for life, as I said. We want no other but the one we first chose. Unless that one is dead."

She groaned, frustrated. "I am not fully your kind. You forget that. I am also my father's daughter, foul soul that he was."

"Perhaps." He grasped his bearded chin between his fingers and stroked. "The elvin blood could complicate matters." Sherak shrugged. "I will check in on you another evening. Lainious knows me as Brother Sherak, should you wonder why I found it so easy to enter this place. The minds of men are easy to twist to our will, Althyn. Another secret you should be advised to remember and be wary of...but I am sure you've noticed the effects already." He frowned and shook his head. "You remember the other mer that wanted you. They will try again to steal you, mate or not. You are valuable among the ones in the sea." He got up, ran his fingers through his hair, and walked out.

She realized then that he was wearing temple robes, like that of a lower priest. His warning bothered her. Could the others do as he had done and come to her bed? She knew she was weak, her body suffering from the poison the vile lizard had infected her with.

Althyn sat up. Her body ached. She felt cold and still so very tired. "Lainious," she called. "Come to me."

She waited for a time, but soon grew impatient. "Lainious!"

The girl at her bedside squeaked and sat up. "Assantra!" She gathered herself and stood, looking startled. "I must have..." The young woman looked around the room, squinting. "I mean, is there something I can get for you?"

"Yes," she grumbled. "Get Lainious. A lot of use you are sleeping there. You're supposed to be watching over me."

"B-but you were asleep. Lainious said I was to weave you stories when you woke." She looked genuinely confused.

"Weave me stories?" Althyn turned her head to the side, regarding the girl with interest. "You are a storyweaver?"

"Oh yes, I am. Would you like to hear a tale now?"

Her anger thinned. She had wanted a storyweaver of her own. Ever since she had heard they existed, she wondered what it would be like to get lost in the words of another. "Yes, of course I would like a story woven for me. But fetch Lainious first. He should be at my side, always."

"Of course, Assantra. As you wish.' The girl hurried to the door and went out in the hall. She left behind a small paper book bound with a cord of leather. Inked symbols covered the parchment. Words. Secrets. Knowledge. Althyn wanted to know what they said. She needed to learn them so that she, too, could weave her own tales, stories of her conquests, songs that her mother had taught to her.

The door opened and Lainious came in, the storyweaver trailing behind him, his hair mussed and his eyes half open. "What is it?" he asked. "Is the antidote working? Are you unwell?"

"I'm cold," she told him. "So very cold."

He nodded and went to the shelves to fetch more blankets. As he spread them across the bed, she watched his unclothed chest, the lean muscles rippling there. His long fingers straightened the coverlets across her. He leaned in and gently laid her back upon the pillows. "You must rest more, Althyn. Sleep will help you return to health. He meant to kill you. It's a good thing I knew what it was he tainted your blood with."

She reached up and set her hand on his shoulder. "Sleep beside me. You're tired. You've no color in your face, and your eyes..."

He nodded and climbed into the bed, settling beside her.

"Udora will tell us a story." He slipped an arm beneath Althyn's body. He was hot, his skin taking the chill away from her almost immediately. But he did not look upon her as he had done before she was with Tolston. His eyes were not as fixated, his voice not as mellow. Still, his expression was one of adoration. Genuine admiration. He had feelings for her even though her usual charms were not working as they had.

Althyn turned on her side, baring her back to his warmth. He set his face against her shoulder, his breathing already slow, steady, as if he were on the verge of sleep.

"Tell me about mermaids," Althyn said to the young woman. "What do you know of them?"

Lainious sighed and breathed in deep, as if he wanted to know the scent of her hair. His other hand slipped around her waist to clasp with the first, so that he embraced her beneath the blankets.

Udora settled herself on the seat by the bed, her small eyes growing wide. "Ah, the mer. I know many tales of the sea people. A sailor from Hareth, on hermitage to this very temple, once told me he was bewitched by such a beauty. Every seventh day he passed the port of Locatia, and there, wading among the rocks, he would spy a dark-haired woman. She would sing gaily, the wind whipping through her thick curls, her face upturned as his ship passed. The sailor's name was Jacques, and he would, at first, wave to the lady. She would raise her hand in return, and continue the haunting melody.

"Jacques was married to a fine wife who bore him two sons and kept his modest house clean. But at night, after loving his wife of ten years, he would lay awake and listen to the sounds of the sea that drifted into his window, and he would hear that dark-haired woman's song. He did not understand the words of it, only that she sang for him, that she wanted him.

"And the next time he passed by her alcove of rocks, he slowed his fishing boat and set his anchor. He watched her sing for hours, beautiful songs that made him want to weep with sorrow or laugh with joy. As he stared across the distance that parted them, she slowly moved closer. The tide was coming in, and it was getting late that day. He feared the water might cast her out to sea and that she might drown.

"'Go back, fair beauty,' he said. 'For I cannot bear to come upon this alcove every seventh day and not find you here singing for me.'"

The woman did not go back. She climbed into his small vessel and appeared to him in her human skin, which she had sewn together with magic. He was so in awe of her beauty that he forgot his wife, his children. He did not think of the nets he had cast that day, or care to find them. Instead, he melted into the mermaid's kisses, and laid his back across the seat of his boat so that she could tease away his clothes and love him beneath the dimming sunlight."

Udora paused, gauging Althyn's face with her stony gray eyes.

Althyn frowned. "That is the end? She seduced him and then what happened? That can't be all there is to it."

"Oh no, there is more." Udora grinned, and Althyn decided there was something mischievous about her, a certain sparkle in her eyes. "By morning, Jacques awoke, his body marked by the lust he had succumbed to all through the night. He stared up at the blue sky above him and wept, for he then remembered that he was a wedded man.

"He sat up and pulled his clothing back on. His lover had left him in the night. As he drew the anchor and manned the sail, he regretted all he had done and vowed he would not come back to the alcove on seventh day again." The storyweaver straightened her back and cleared her throat.

Althyn wondered what would happen then. She felt Lainious's breath on her neck, warm, and steady, for he had long since fallen asleep. "Did he go back to his wife?"

"He did, Assantra. He returned to her in shame, but he could not bear to hurt her, so he stayed away from their bed and lied, saying that he had taken ill at sea and did not want to share his illness with her. His wife, never having had a reason to doubt him, made him a bed in the main room of the house and let him stay there beneath the covers to regain his health. She tended him and worried, for she truly loved her husband.

"When he was certain his love bites were faded, he returned to his usual bed and his wife's arms, but he could not love her. His body would not awaken to her touch. When his wife kissed him, or ran her fingers along him, it was the mermaid's face he saw, the mermaid's song he heard. He did the best he could to pleasure his wife, but he could not do it as he had done before."

"She stole his virility?"

"Of course." Udora half smiled before she went on. "Jacques did as he had vowed. He avoided the alcove of his transgression and sailed another way each seventh day. He thought perhaps he had dreamed up the woman, for he had never seen anyone so lovely to behold. He began to put her out of his mind, and soon believed he *had* made up the lover from the sea.

"Eleven moon cycles passed. Jacques had let his lover slip from his mind. The sea was wild that seventh day, churning and angry and trying its best to capsize his boat. He knew he needed to get to the nearest shore, but he was closest to the alcove where he used to pause, and he didn't think it wise to go that way."

The wind had picked up outside, and Althyn heard it blowing through the cracks of the wood that Lainious had set in the broken window frame. The storyweaver's expression was changing now, her eyes narrowing, her smile fading.

"The ocean pushed his boat to the rocks nonetheless. His little vessel was tossed against the jagged peaks until it smashed into five pieces. Jacques swam as best he could while rain pounded him from above and the sea slapped at his back. He was pulled under and resurfaced, kicking his legs as hard as he could. The rocks scraped at his arms and legs, cutting into his skin until he smelled his own blood mingled with the salty water."

She leaned forward then. "He prayed for some miracle from the old gods, but they did not answer him. Instead, he heard a sad song on the wind, his sea lover's voice drifting like a banshee's cry through the tumultuous storm. He felt he had no choice but to follow that sound. As he swam in the direction he thought he heard her coming from, he found that the waves were calmer, that he could soon touch the sand with his feet. Near the shore, he caught sight of his sea lover, a bundle swathed in cloth held close to her breast. She was naked save for her dark hair, which covered much of her like a cloak. When she saw him, she held up one hand like old times.

"At that moment, the sea dragged him backward, away from her. He knew he would die then. He had done an evil to break the marriage vow between him and his wife, and this was his punishment. He let the water cover his face. He breathed in its taste and let the liquid fill his lungs. He could not go to shore and face that woman, no matter how beautiful she was. Nor could he return to his wife after this day. She deserved a better man. One who would not stray from her as he had done.

"Just as he was about to lose himself to the darkness of death, he felt hands on his body, pulling him up, higher and higher, until his face was pushed to the surface. He felt the curve of her breasts against his body and he knew it was his sea lover, his musical temptress come to save him from certain death. But how? How could she swim through such dangerous waters when he could not? How could she be strong enough to bear him, as she was doing, to the safety of the beach?"

"The mer are strong," Althyn whispered, suddenly proud of this tale. That mermaid had wanted that man and taken him. She had spared him from death and would claim him again on that stormy beach. She liked this story.

Udora only nodded. "She dragged him to safety and knelt beside him while he coughed out all he had swallowed. She was sad, tears pooling in her sea-colored eyes..." Udora squinted. "Eyes just like yours, Assantra."

That only pleased Althyn all the more.

"'Why do you cry?' he asked her.

"'You did not return to me, and now...' The woman waved a hand at the lower part of her body, which was no longer human as it had been when he'd loved her in his boat. She was a monster, her fish tail all that remained of what had been legs when he had spied her on the beach only a short time ago. 'I cannot return to the land. My human skin is lost, swallowed by the sea when I came to rescue you. Our child will die now unless you care for him. He does not have a merskin as I do, for he was born of us when I was your kind. He is human, like you, his father.'"

Althyn bit her lip, intrigued, but disbelieving now. She could be mer or gryphon, perhaps anything she chose. Her cousin had said mer were shape-shifters. And her blood was not pure, but she could go back to the shape of her mother's kind when it pleased her.

"So Jacques swore he would care for the child. He waited out the storm, the small baby in his arms now, fast asleep and fitting against him as if he had carried the babe many times before. He watched his sea lover vanish into the dark waters, and sadly, he walked along the shore until he reached his village and then his home.

"His wife asked him whose child it was. He lied and said that its mother had perished shortly after the ship she'd been in crashed to the shore, as his had done. That he had promised her before her last breath that he would care for the little one as if he were his own. And so it was that he raised his lovechild beneath his wife's eyes, and he could never make another child after that. Nor was he happy. When the child was only three moon cycles, his wife left him for the want of a man who could please her in lovemaking. She did not even take the children she had made with Jacques.

"When Jacques grew old and his three sons became of an age to set sail and fish, he stayed home and did not go to the sea with them. Instead, he stood on the dock and tried to sing the songs his sea lover had always warmed his heart with. One seventh day, he threw himself into the water and did not come back to the surface."

Althyn crinkled her brow. "He killed himself because he could not have her?"

"Yes."

She chewed her bottom lip and shook her head. "Foolish man."

"That is the meaning of the story, that Jacques was a fool to be lured by the woman when he had a wife already. He should not have listened to her song. He should not have stopped in the alcove."

Althyn shook her head. "He could not help himself. A man is powerless in such instances."

"Powerless?" Udora looked curious. "Why do you say that?"

"It is the way of things. Men can't fight the lure of a mer. She will get him if he is what she wants. He has no choice in the matter."

Udora nodded. "Perhaps that is right."

"It was a good story." Althyn closed her eyes and yawned. "Tomorrow you will tell me another like that. A story with a lover and the sea. I like stories with such things. And riches. Gold and jewels. Sparkling treasures to be discovered and kept."

"Of course, Assantra. I will tell you such stories any time you wish it."

Althyn smiled before she went to sleep, the story of the unfortunate fisherman and the mermaid spinning through her dreams.

Chapter Twenty-One
Called to the Sea

MORNING CAME AND Althyn felt the gentle touch of fingers running back and forth along her arm. She didn't need to open her eyes to see who it was.

"Are you hungry?" Lainious asked.

"Yes." The thought of food woke her stomach to grumbling.

"I'll get something for you to eat. Stay here, though. The lines from the poison are faded, but moving around will do nothing to help it leave your system."

She reached out and found his hand before he could leave. Althyn opened her eyes and stared at him. He was still as attractive as he had been that day she'd first seen him on the island. His hair was combed through. He had dressed himself in fresh clothes. But she noticed she did not feel the same way as she had then. "A man came to me last night," she told him. "A priest who called himself Brother Sherak."

"Yes. He found me on the beach when I was gathering the anemones and followed me through the jungle, helping me find the roots for your antidote."

"That man is no priest. He's my cousin, or so he says. Next time he tries to see me, don't let him in."

He looked confused. "Did he say something to upset you?"

She shook her head. "I don't trust him. That's all. I don't trust many...men."

"All right. I will do as you say."

She nodded, forcing a wan smile. "And I will speak with my uncle this morning. Wake him and bring him here to me."

"Yes, of course."

She released his wrist and watched him take his leave. The storyweaver was gone. Her book sat on the chair by the bed.

Althyn pushed herself up against the many pillows at the rear of the massive bed. She studied the room, thinking it a fine place. There were not enough weapons on her wall. She would need to acquire more...more than Tolston had in his chamber.

Tolston. She thought of his face, of his rough beard scratching against her chin when they kissed. She hardly knew him, only that he was cruel and a steadfast lover. She would know his scent in the dark, and she breathed deep, smelling it faintly on the linens. It was mingled with Lainious' scent too, but that didn't bother her. She licked her lips and wished for some water to drink. Lying in bed did not suit her. She wanted to get up. *To recapture my lover.* Yes, that idea appealed to her. He needed to be brought back. He needed to be at her side. There was no reason he should run from her now. So what if there was a child? If he was her true mate, he would have remained.

Lainious returned with a tray of bread and cheese. There were fruits she did not know and juice with a small cup of water. She ate her fill and stared at him as he watched her from beside the bed.

"I will have Tolston back." She swallowed down the last of the juice. "When I am well again, I will take the ship to Truias and find him."

Lainious frowned and looked away. 'If that is your wish, mistress."

"It is."

"But wait until your body has recovered from the poison."

She hissed. "I will have that priest's head, too. How dare he attack me? How dare he steal that dagger?"

Lainious returned his attention to her, his eyes plaintive. "Perhaps you should consider the temple. You stood before the people. You held their sacred blade. You spoke with the voice of their god. They believe you are the Assantra of Othia now, their leader. For what you have ordered, the release and return of the slave children..."

She snorted. "What are you saying? That I should stay here forever? That I should let him go and find some other woman to warm his bed?" Her voice became shrill and frightening.

He swallowed, nervous.

"He's mine!" She pushed the tray from her lap. "Like you, like my uncle, like my father's soul trapped in that axe I killed him with! Tolston is mine, and I will have him back. I will have what I want!"

He reached for the tray and lifted it clear from her path. "You have a rage in you...like your father did. I fear you as I love you, Althyn. I fear what you could do, what you have done...what you are."

"You *should* fear me." She fisted the coverlet in her hands. "All who see me should fear me." Her chest heaved with her temper. A tingle singed her body, and she laid back, weary. "I am a dangerous creature. Powerful.'

Lainious nodded and backed away. "I know."

She waited until he had left before she closed her eyes. She didn't feel those things she had said. She felt tired and weak. Sick from the poison and drained. Most of all, a dark, biting loneliness had settled in her. An emptiness that was threatening to eat up her mind. She needed Tolston. She must have him.

Light footsteps.

She raised her head.

Her uncle had come, his eyes puffy with darkness beneath them. He looked more bedraggled than usual, dirtier, if that were possible. When he stood over her, she smelled the drink he had been consuming. A flask of it was hooked into his belt. "I thought you might die."

She sighed. "No. I'm too strong to die." She patted the bed. "Sit, Uncle. I have something I want you to do for me."

He seated himself and took her hand in his. "Anything you ask."

"I want you to look over this temple for me. Take stock of its riches. Be sure they are protected from any that might want to steal them. When I am well enough, I will go back to Truias. There is something there I need."

"No, no," he said. "They will hunt you there. Lord Salak's relatives..."

"I will kill them if they stand in my way."

He groaned and shook his head. "Tell me what is it you want and I will fetch it for you."

"I want the high guard. I want Tolston."

Anthis arched an eyebrow. "You wish me to capture him? To bring him here to you?"

"No. I'll do it. I'll not have you thrown in their tower again."

He made a nervous laugh. "There are other men here, Althyn. Men who are strong and handsome. You could have your choosing of them. You do understand that?" His voice had dropped to a whisper, one that sounded riddled with uncertainty.

"I want Tolston."

He nodded. "You remind me so much of your mother." Sadness filled his eyes with tears. He hastily wiped his arm across them to hide it. "She would have no other than your father. And we both know why you shouldn't have wanted him."

"I'm stronger than my mother was."

He nodded. "Stay here then. If he wants you, he'll come back for you."

Her eyes narrowed. "If he wants me? It doesn't matter what *he* wants." She crossed her arms over her chest.

Anthis nodded, but his face had paled as if he had seen something dangerous and frightening. "I'll look after the temple for you. That much I am capable of."

"Good. Now leave me to rest." She watched him walk out, but not before he cast a mournful look back at her.

Althyn napped for most of the day. She drank two more draughts of Lainious's concoction to counter the poison in her system. The times she slept, he lay beside her, his body warm and comfortable against her own. Their routine went on for five days with no word from Tolston or attacks from Truias, and a steady stream of notes from the little town. Scraps of cloth or parchments thanking her for the children. Always the children.

"You are a wise Assantra," the storyweaver said on the sixth morning. "The people love you. They revere you. To have given them back what the temple took without asking was a brilliant choice."

Althyn gritted her teeth. "What use do I have for children?" she said under her breath, irritated by another pile of notes that Lainious was setting beside her.

He smiled and sat to read them aloud. As his words drifted through the room, she heard another sound, far away, the sound of a man's voice singing. The words were her mother's tongue. She found the song soothing, the cadence familiar.

"Be silent, Lainious," she snapped. "Can you not hear that?"

"I hear nothing." He looked around, clearly bewildered. After setting his hand on her forehead, he pursed his lips.

"My cousin comes for me again." She pushed up from the pillows and struggled to escape the bed. As she hastily pulled on a silken robe against Lainious' protests, she noticed that the voice indeed was drawing closer. "You will keep him from me!"

"Of course. As you wish." Lainious hurried to her door and opened it.

Althyn eyed the boarded up window. She looked at the curtain over the old opening through which she had entered the chamber for the first time. Sherak was coming, but how would he get to her this time?

She heard a commotion in the hall. Lainious shouted for someone to be gone, that she did not want to see him. But then her door opened and her cousin strolled in as easily as if he owned the temple. She backed to the wall that bore her sword, and now a few trifle weapons Lainious had brought to her as gifts.

"What do you want?"

Sherak's mouth twisted into a sideways grimace. "Such distrust. Have I done something to anger you?" He pushed back the hood he wore to reveal his face. A purple bruise stood out by his left eye and a series of gashes as if claws had rent his cheek.

"I don't want to go to the sea. I don't want to kill the mate I took, and I damn well don't want you here telling me lies to coerce me to your will."

He snorted out a laugh and seated himself by the dressing table. "I only came to see if you were well. You look better, cousin. Stronger." He picked at his nails as if he were uninterested in her at the moment. "But I believe a child still grows within your womb. A shame. A little mongrel. What world will it find peace in?" He raised his chin and seared her with a cold glare. "You belong with our kind, with the mer. They need you now in the depths. They need a queen, an heir. The wars rage below. Chaos has gripped the reef. You will soon see the fruits of such madness here on the mainland."

She shrugged. "It is no concern of mine!"

"Ah, but it is." He rolled his head to crack his neck. She noticed more wounds upon him. A scratch near his jugular. A red mark on the back of his hand.

"Who did that to you?" She nodded at him.

He snarled when he spoke, his pink lips revealing his fangs. She saw that there was blood streaked in his beard as well. "Lotias. We fought when I came to the shore. He followed me, taking on the shape of a land walker and cursing me for doing so."

She leaned back against the wall, her sword close enough to take if need be. "Lotias. One of the ones who tried to claim me beneath the sea."

Sherak nodded. His face became a fierce visage. "But he will not claim you. He will not touch you again."

"You killed him?"

He smiled, his sharp teeth strangely alluring to her. "Oh yes. I killed him and tore his body to pieces to feed the sea's hunger."

"Oh." She reached back and did grip the sword's handle then. "Have you come now to kill me?"

His brow crinkled. Sea green eyes flashed with confusion. "Kill you? Never. I wish to serve you. Can you not see that?"

She lifted the blade from the wall and held it with both hands. It was long and awkward, but light, too light to be man-made. "Maybe I should kill you. I still distrust you."

He shrugged. "If it would please my princess to kill me, then I am hers to dispose of." Sherak stood and strolled across the room. He knelt before her and looked up, awaiting her decision.

She hissed out an exasperated sigh. "You puzzle me."

He smiled.

"I tire of this room, of being in bed."

"Come to the sea with me this night. We will swim together and chase the tide. I will tell you of your enemies. I will show you the world you deny." He raised himself up and held his hand out, beckoning to her. "Come."

"I am not yet healed of the poison."

"It will never leave you wholly."

She groaned. "Why not?"

"Like your sword, it will always be at your side...a curse as much as a blessing. Although I see no blessing in the poison other than to teach you that you are not invincible."

She shook her head. "You speak in riddles."

"No. I do not."

His hand closed over hers and he urged her to lower the weapon. "This sword has been passed down for many generations in our line. It will find its heir should she be lost or if it is parted from her. Like two mates drawn to each other, it cannot be parted from its true wielder very long." He tapped a red jewel in the hilt. "There are many kinds of magic instilled in its keeping. This jewel will heal, should you ask it. This"—he tapped a blue one—"will call ice. This one will call fire." He leaned in close to her until his forehead touched with hers. "The blade has a name. Protector of the Queen in the humans' tongue. A king had it fashioned in the underworld for his bride so that she might fight in the wars and never be weakened by use of her own magic." His eyes held her mesmerized, green, so deep and perilous to look upon. He possessed the same luring gaze that she had.

"Heal me, my princess. Set your hand to this jewel and ask that it be done. Speak in your mother's tongue. Surely she taught you that much."

"She taught me only songs."

He moaned. "Yes. Sing then. Sing what she would sing when your father hurt her. Sing those words and ask the magic to heal me."

"But I can heal you without the sword."

"At the price of your strength, and you are still weak from your wound."

She gritted her teeth and growled. "Fine." Althyn stared into his eyes and sang the song her mother had taught her, remembering how she would rock back and forth on the floor, her face bruised and her heart so broken and empty. Red light glittered around them. She felt a whoosh of air engulf her and circle them.

Sherak grimaced as if it pained him. His eyes fluttered. "It is done, cousin."

She watched the gash above his beard close over. Looking down, the same happened on his injured hand. And he was right. She didn't feel a rush of fatigue as she had when she had healed Lainious or removed his scars. She felt better, as if the blade had worked its healing on her as well.

"Your mother was wrong to keep her secrets from you." His hands pried the blade from her hold, and he set it back upon its hook on the wall. "I will teach you to be mer. Come."

"I will not come like a slave at your word."

"I ask you as a humble servant, as your protector and sworn follower. I ask you so that you might know what lies in the underworld. What treasures you forsake by not claiming them."

"Treasures?"

"Yes, Althyn." He closed his hand over hers, and she took a tentative step with him toward the door. Another. They walked past Lainious, who lay prone on the floor, past the rooms beyond hers, and through the labyrinth of the temple.

"What did you do to Lainious?"

"He sleeps. I would not harm your slave." He kept walking, leading her away. "You have done much here in this land of man and gods. Think of what is possible among your own kind."

"I imagine it is the same. With fools standing in positions of power who need only have their heads cut off to end their reign."

Sherak laughed. "You are quite right. Only Thenai stands in the way of your claim. And to take what should be yours, you must end him. Claim your right as queen."

"And take you as my mate?"

He paused.

They stood beside an indoor garden. The plants were laden with ripe fruits and women went about tending them. The sweet scent of flowers filled the air. When the women took notice of her, they bowed low and nodded their deference.

"You have a mate whose child you carry even now."

"But that's what you want, isn't it? You want me. You've come here to steal me as the others would have."

He squeezed her hand. "It is not what *you* desire." Sherak walked on, and she kept pace with him.

Each room of priestesses they passed offered her another glimpse of the high regard with which she was held. Bows, whispers of praise, eyes filled with wonder and awe. She liked the feeling it gave her. As if she were a goddess to be worshipped.

"They revere you already. You like this. You need to rule. Were made to be a queen." Sherak smiled, pleased with his observation. "In time, the mer will treat you as these humans do."

When they reached the wide arch that led from the temple to the village below, Althyn stopped and looked back at the place she was about to leave. Vines curled in and around the stone pillars that supported the arch. Small, white flowers perfumed the entrance, making it seem ethereal. Yet, it was not. Here was a place of power, of solitude, if she so chose. She had made a home for herself in the few days she had been here. The sun was high above, shining down upon her skin and warming her body. She recalled what it felt like when she had held the Othian Dagger, what it had made her say and do. Something from beyond this world had touched her soul at that moment and tried to control it.

"Are the gods real?" she asked.

"As real as you and I. They seldom intervene when they should. We are nothing but entertainment to them. Shun their presence and you will survive well enough without them." He let go of her hand and rolled his shoulders as if loosening his body would improve his countenance. "Accept them into your life, and they will rule it."

"And if I accept you into my life?"

His eyes narrowed. "You are wary. That's good. You have little trust in others, but I swear you can lay your trust in me."

"What do you gain?"

"Your attentions if I succeed. Death if I fail. At the least, one of us will kill Thenai and set the seas into the hands of our line again."

She pulled her hand from his to cross her arms over her chest. "You killed the other one. Why not this one?"

He scoffed and pointed to the sea. "And how will I draw him to me? Would you have me shift into your shape and bare my chest so that he might be fooled into claiming me?"

She smirked. "It sounds like a good enough plan."

Sherak seemed to contemplate the idea's merits for a time. He looked to the sea and then back to the temple. "No. I think he would see through the ruse. Besides, you are mated. That will surely anger him enough to distraction."

She turned her back on him. "I am your bait. That's all."

"Yes, you are. But I do this for you." He wound his arm about her waist and tugged her into a walk again. They journeyed along the path toward the village. "You can't tell me you don't long for a battle, that you don't want to taste the blood in the water."

She did want that. She craved it as much as she craved having Tolston back.

Chapter Twenty-Two
Thenai of the Underworld

THE VILLAGE WAS poor. There were fish hanging to dry along lines. Nets for mending were cast by the wood scrap fences, and people were not tarrying. They worked at their chores, mending homes, tending goats, grinding grain, or planting in their small gardens. All took notice of Althyn, though. Dressed as she was in only a night robe, she likely made a strange sight. But they knew her name and called her by the title, Assantra. Some held up a hand to wave at her. A few thrust forth a child and smiled, thanking her for what she had done.

Sherak nodded at them, hurrying onward past the hovels and tiny shops to the span of white beach and the many docks. There were no ships there at this hour, for they were all at sea, fishing.

"Come now. We'll swim for a time. The sea will do your body good." He led her to a stand of beach grass where they both cast their clothes off. He was handsome in his human shape. He, too, appraised her with his eyes.

"You are even more lovely nude in the light of the day."

She shrugged. "Am I to lure Thenai now, or do we play games in the waves for a time?"

He reached for her hand. His fingers curled with hers. With a smile, he said, "Games in the waves. Thenai will come if he hears you sing to the sea. In fact, he waits for your voice, as I have done."

Althyn frowned. She followed her cousin into the cool water. Goosebumps prickled her skin and tautened her nipples. She breathed deep and tasted the salt in the air. It was familiar and comforting. It was her other home. They waded in, and she willed her body to make its change. Dipping beneath the water filled her with a renewed sense of strength. She swam alongside Sherak as if they had always done so, perfectly matched in time and pace.

"*I will show you the city where I was born, where your mother lived when she was young.*"

She nodded. This excited her curiosity. She knew nothing about her mother's past. They swam over a thick, brown reef rent with all manner of sea life. Schools of silvery fish passed by, their bodies slices of light in the dim water. Despite the darkness, she could see far before her. She tasted the distinct scents of the other creatures that lived in the water. And she recognized Sherak's flavor, as well.

A great monster with a jaw full of jagged teeth circled above them. Sherak took Althyn's hands and spun with her through the water. Faster and faster they moved, their tails in unison, their bodies facing each other. "*The agda will eat us if it catches us.*" His voice was a stern warning in her mind.

Through darkness and shadows he brought her until they came to a city of sorts. The cave-like homes were carved into the coral bed. Plants waved at them in a rainbow of colors. Sherak dipped, taking her with him into one of the holes. She stiffened, thinking he wanted to keep her captive here, but the cave gave way to the wonders he had hinted at. The stolen treasures of land walkers had been piled high within the secret place. Gems and jewelry, coins and metal boxes, weapons, so many weapons. Her eyes widened over it all, and she wanted it to be hers.

"*This pleases you?*"

"*Yes.*"

"*Strange that you desire the weapons so much. You covet your mother's blade. You've even started a collection on the wall by that bed in the temple. It is usual for the females of our kind to collect trinkets, shiny things that sparkle in the rays of light that filter from the surface. But it has always been a male's way to desire things that cause death.*"

"*I like them because they offer power over life.*"

He gave a curt nod. "*They are but tools. You will find that, among our kind, weapons such as these are merely for show. It is the words with which we speak and the way in which we dominate those beneath us that make us powerful or not.*"

She liked the sound of that. Dominate. She would dominate them all, make them bow to her and serve her. If they did not, she would kill them.

Sherak flashed his sharp-toothed smile again. "*The sea appeals to you. It speaks to the part of you that was spawned from the underworld. You could be happy beneath the waves with us.*"

"*I could be happy walking above with my mate.*"

His smile faded. He didn't seem to like that statement at all.

"*Where are the others?*" She swam away from him to peek out from the cave they had entered. Surely, he couldn't be the only merman here. There were so many other caves, so many that might also hold riches as this one did.

"*They are likely fighting Thenai's ranks. If the wars continue, we will lose our hold here in time. Thenai must be stopped.*"

"*Then stop him!*" She glared at him over her shoulder. "*It is not such a difficult thing to take a life.*"

His face curled in disgust. He joined her side and took her hand in his. "*You truly are not like the females of the underworld.*"

She tugged her hand free and swam out to see what other wonders were hidden in the darkness. Each cave she entered was similar to the first. Some held weapons, others great vases filled with coins. There was even one piled with a collection of bones. "*It is in our nature to collect. Interesting.*"

Sherak watched over her with an arched eyebrow, clearly intrigued. "*And what will you collect, Althyn? More weapons for your temple wall?*"

She smirked and flapped her tail, sending her body flying out of the dim cave of bones. Faster and faster she swam toward the surface. The thought she sent back to him made him choke out a startled sound.

"*Oh no. I will collect followers. Every person loyal to Othia will bow to me. Every town, every village, all in time will send me tithes and worship me as their goddess. Every mer beneath the waves will know I am their queen.*"

She emerged near the island and pulled her fishlike body up onto a smooth rock. Waves crashed against the stone and sprayed froth upon her shining scales. She traced the intricate shapes and wondered at all that she could become if only she dared to try. A sea serpent, a minotaur, a terrible dragon that breathed fire like the one her uncle spoke of in his tales.

Sherak broke the surface and held his place beneath her. "Let me conquer the mer now," she whispered, and flashed a mischievous grin. "Oh, I will have my rein over this underworld and all its treasures. There is no need to wait." She ran her hand a final time over one moist, scaled hip and willed the change to come. Tail to legs and feet. Bits of fish skin and blots of blood filtered away with each wave splashed. When it was complete, she stood and pushed her wet hair back from her shoulders. Althyn opened her mouth and sang to the waves. She sang to her lost race and to the one merman out there who would have her as his own. Her voice carried far and wide until gulls answered and flew overhead in a swarm. Fish leaped from the water and slipped back in as if answering her call.

Not long after she began, great sea beasts, whales, and dolphins peered up from their safe vantage, crested the waves, and then flashed their tails as they again descended. Something profound would happen. She felt it.

Sherak merely watched and waited, his green eyes growing darker, his expression more bloodthirsty. He wanted a fight as much as she wanted another set of followers to rule.

Her voice became a sonorous lure reverberating across the sea. When she saw the creature she had called finally rise up from the water, she did not stop. She couldn't. It was an addiction, a way to control. She loved the way it made her feel. So alive. So dangerous.

Sherak turned and frowned at the approaching rival. Althyn smiled and sang.

Thenai swam to the stones, his face stern, his beard knotted with sea plants, and his eyes dark and cold. He was not the same kind as Sherak. It was obvious. And he was much older and more muscular.

"Be silent." He shook a fist at her.

Althyn's song broke into a bout of lilting laughter. "You have no right to order my silence. If I wish to sing until the world ends its days, then I will do so."

"You don't know your place." He moved closer, bypassing her cousin, though it was obvious he knew Sherak waited there. "You belong in the underworld. You belong in the arms of a strong lover, a leader who will keep your wiles at bay and your sharp little tongue busy." When he reached the edge of the stones, he stopped and looked her up and down. He sniffed the air and curled his upper lip. "You have the scent of man upon you."

She laughed at him. "You have the scent of seaweed and rotten fish upon you."

His dark eyes flashed with anger. "Insolent. Disrespectful."

"Sure of myself and what is mine," she taunted. "Even you belong to me." She waved a hand at him. "Come upon this stone and try to claim me. I dare you."

Sherak edged closer.

Thenai hissed between his sharp teeth. "It is you who must come." He slapped at the water. "Claim the sea as yours. Defeat me if you dare. Lotias is no more, and I will kill Sherak, as well, leaving only the two of us as heirs. Then you will keep my burrow well decorated with your shining hair and fanciful ears."

She snorted. "I will kill you this day. And any that dare to stand before me..."

Thenai lunged. His thick, wet fingers locked over her ankle. He tugged. She slipped and tumbled forward. In moments, her anger at being tripped surged to the forefront of her conscience. She felt the gryphon part of her trying to take over, but a creature that needed air would be no match for the burly merman. She needed to be something of the sea, something dangerous and able to breathe in the underworld.

Her skin rippled and grew cold. He dragged her beneath the surface, choking off her air. Prickles shot down her spine. His other hand took her calf and he pulled her down further. But his grip soon slipped over the smooth surface of her now leathery skin. Her mouth hurt when the teeth within lengthened. Her arms became wide fins, her legs pulled together into one lengthy, fin-tipped appendage. It felt stronger than the tail of a mer. She whipped it sideways and Althyn shot forth when her tail butted against Thenai's head.

She looked back and saw him floundering. A cloud of blood drifted from his temple. But his eyes held hers, changed as she was. She had become the agda, the sea monster that would have eaten her and Sherak earlier. And her stomach grumbled for the taste of meat.

She shot toward him, her maw wide and ready to receive his flesh.

He darted to the side, narrowly escaping her attack.

If the mer were shape-shifters, she wondered why he did not take advantage of the talent. Was it pride? Shock? Or were not all able to shift so freely?

She slapped her tail and glided at him. This time, his arm caught in her teeth. Althyn bit down. Blood warmed her monster's tongue and she found she could not resist the urge to shake her head violently.

A garbled scream echoed in the water and in her mind. She didn't stop, but bit again...and again, eating him piece by piece until the hunger stopped and the sea was a dark place colored red with death. There was naught left of Thenai but shreds of gore that floated out to the fish waiting to snap them up.

When Sherak swam toward her, she could hardly resist the urge to tear him apart as well. He would taste like the first one. Better maybe since he was not as old and tough.

"*The queen has taken her place among us.*"

His words echoed beneath the sea, spreading out to any mer that might take notice of the declaration. *And I am a queen to be feared,* she thought with a dagger-toothed agda grin. *A queen like no race above or below has ever seen.*

Chapter Twenty-Three
The Servant and the Mate

ALTHYN SWAM FOR a long while in her taken form, surveying the underworld and silently laying claim to all she saw. When she swept over the caves they had explored before, she took on the shape of her mother's kin, and felt less angry, less hungry, or apt to strike out. The mer did not come to her, and she accepted that as a sign of their subservience. They slunk across the lower reef, their silhouettes flashes of darkness that could be mirages. But she knew they were real enough.

Sherak swam close to her, but always a head behind, not as he had done before. He called to the others in his own tongue, little of which she understood. It didn't take knowledge of his language to know that he was proclaiming her queen and bragging about what she had done. She puffed out her chest and looked down her nose at the others. Weak. They were all nothing compared to her. She would control them, will them to do her bidding as she willed her body to change with her ever shifting moods.

She spied a greater city beyond the grouping of caves. A silver towered gathering of carved stones. There the mer were not as fearful. They floated before the circular entrances of their homes, some of the men holding sharpened spears, the women bedecked in shining jewels. They were Thenai's kind. The colors they shared with the deceased warrior matched. At first, none moved, but slowly, they deferred to her. Men nodded with a flick of their chins. Women raised one hand in salute.

They were hers now. All of them. *Mine,* she thought. Could there be no end to what she was capable of doing?

On and on through the night and the next day, Sherak showed her the reach of the underworld. There were other kinds of mer. Seal-bodied creatures that had no fangs, and softer shapes. Mer with tails that curled in on themselves and glittered like gold. Those ones watched her with beady, black eyes that never blinked. Mer with serpent tails, mer with doubled fish tails, mer that were not quite human-looking at all. They watched her with fearful reverence, webbed hands waving but once as she passed.

There was no need for a speech to this congregation. Sherak enlightened them all.

When she tired of surveying, she swam for the surface. Sherak followed, something like Lainious, only not as yielding or kind. Her cousin was hardened and blunt. They both broke the surface and she watched the top of the sun slowly rising in the distance.

"Will you stay with us now, my queen?"

Far in the distance, she saw a ship with its sails wide. The wind was catching it up and forcing it onward. She felt like that ship. The need to move forward pushed at her. The need to find her mate and have him back at her side niggled at the back of her thoughts.

"Will you?" he repeated.

"In time. When I have taken all that I care to have from the land. Only then will I return wholly to the sea. For now, I go to Truias and my mate. I will win him over as well."

Sherak shot her a stern glance. "Or you will kill him in trying to bend him to your will. It's different with a mate, Althyn. Different for them than it is with any male you would seduce simply for the pleasure of wooing their simple minds. When you choose a mate, when you give your body over to him, a part of you becomes his. He is not so easily enraptured or controlled. Instinct should drive him from you, because a mermaid, in all her beauty, is a dangerous creature when she is with child."

"I was dangerous before this child you speak of."

His brow rose, and his eyes rounded. "That, I believe with all my heart."

SHE RETURNED TO the mainland and found the nightdress she had left among the plants. Sherak watched her from his vantage in the waves, his face a silvery silhouette in the churning sea. He would not come with her to the temple, nor to the port town of Truias she planned to revisit. But she knew all she had to do was sing and he would come to her from the sea, if she had need of him.

As she padded along the beach and returned to the winding path that would lead her to the temple, she thought of Tolston. He was so much like her father, his arrogance plain. She knew so little about him, and even what she did know was not inspiring. He used women for his pleasures. He stole from the merchants in the port town. He had even stolen from her.

The people in the village waved and called to her as she bypassed them, distracting her. She needed to be back in the bedchamber, back in the company of her servant. Lainious would prepare her things for travel. She would take the sword, if need be. And her manservant would tend to her as he always did with such care and patience.

Thinking of Lainious calmed her. He was no battle, no test to her power or fury. She traveled up the mountain path and through the many arches while she pondered him. He asked nothing of her, demanded nothing. She could easily take him with her when she chose to depart. Lainious was little trouble. As well, he was good at warming her bed in the night. Sleeping beside another was a rarity that she enjoyed, not that he should be told such a thing.

She clenched her fists as she entered the temple's main gateway. No one questioned her authority here. It was as if she had always ruled this place, and she always would.

Remembering the way, she returned to her bedchamber to find Lainious sitting by the bed, his face pinched with worry. "Where were you?"

"In the sea," she snipped in answer. "It's no concern of yours where I go or what I do. I had things to attend to. Prepare my clothes and my sword. I wish to return to Truias and reclaim my mate."

He frowned. "You should have another draught of the antidote. You should have drank it last night. Traveling is not a safe plan of action at the moment."

She plopped onto the bed and lay back beside him, waving away his warning. "I feel well enough."

"The poison the priest gave you was made from scorpion venom. It stays in your body and kills off your senses little by little, until you feel nothing." He bent over and looked down at her with his beautiful blue eyes. "Will you drink the antidote now?"

She reached up and patted his cheek. "Yes, yes. Give me your potion." Her hand dropped back to the bed. "I feel fine, though. I don't think I need it."

He sighed. Lainious pushed up from the bed and went to the dressing table. There he swirled the concoction with a stirring stick. "Were you swimming?" he asked, offering it to her.

She sat up and took the cup, nodding. "Yes. I swam all through the night."

"You're a mermaid, aren't you?"

She shrugged. "Mostly." The potion tasted as nasty as it had before, thick and bitter. She swallowed it down and grimaced.

"Your mother was. Your father knew that about her. We all knew it, too. It was obvious from the way he couldn't stand to be away from the island for very long. Like he was drawn back against his will and, once he got what he had come for, he left, only to lose his mind until he returned again. He was like a man obsessed with drink, only worse. There was no stopping him."

"You speak of what I already know."

"Yes, I'm sorry." He took her emptied cup away. "I only wanted to ask..."

"Ask what?"

"Is that what it will be like for you and...Tolston." He ground out the other man's name with clear disgust. "Will he keep returning to you like your father did to your mother?"

She chewed her lower lip, thinking. "Maybe that's the way it's meant to be. What would you know of such things anyway? You're only a slave. You've never been with a woman. You said so yourself."

"Right." He clenched his jaw and a muscle in his cheek tightened. "What would I know of love," he said softly. "Only that I feel it for you, and if I were Tolston, I would not have left your side. I will never leave you."

She scoffed, dismissing his confession, and held the empty cup out to him.

He set it on the bedside table.

"It's true," he said and climbed upon the bed beside her. "But maybe that's not what you want." He crawled up until he was over her, staring down at her with intensity. His subservience was missing, his face stern, his eyes set. "Maybe you want your lover to treat you as he will. Maybe you want to be hurt like your mother was."

She glared up at him. "You know nothing of what I want."

"Don't I? You've told me as much. Told me what you want from *me*." His hand caught her wrist when she made to slap him. He forced her arm down into the pillows. She reached with the other, but he did the same, holding her in place. "You want a man who's in control. You want a man who will argue with you. Fight you. *Challenge* you." His face dipped to hers until he was a breath away.

She stared at his mouth, wondering if he would try to kiss her. What had come over her servant? Since she had been with Tolston, the magical hold over Lainious had waned, but he still seemed to be attracted to her, now more than ever and with a fervor she didn't understand.

His tongue flicked out to wash over his lips, wetting them. Then, he parted his lips and crushed her mouth with a fiery kiss. Her mind awakened to every sensation of his body against hers, his weight, his alluring scent, his arousal thick in his pants as he pressed into her. He squeezed her wrists tight when she tried to push him away. He tasted her. Althyn met his advance, kissing back so suddenly that he groaned. Their kiss lingered until her resistance went numb. Why had she wanted Tolston? Why, when Lainious had been there all along, loyal, gentle and kind? And now that he was asserting himself, what was she to do about it?

Lainious raised up, leaving her mouth to look down at her. "If he tries to hurt you, I'll kill him. I promise you that. I'll follow you to Truias, if you want me with you, but I will not stay my hand if he raises his to you."

She breathed out a sigh. When had he become so protective? And why? This was not the same man that she had first met on the ship, the quiet, demure, but handsome slave who waited on her and fashioned sandals. Something had changed inside him.

"You're jealous."

His blue eyes narrowed, roving across her face. "Yes." He ground himself once against her body before he released her and pushed away from the bed. The teasing gesture ignited her lust, but she fought the desire to chase after him.

Althyn lay still, watching him cross the room with the empty cup. He cleaned up the items he'd used to mix her antidote and set them on a tray to be carried away. With a backwards glance, he made for the door to leave. "I'll prepare your things and have the ship readied to leave."

She didn't know whether to call him back or to scream her defiance at him for what he had dared to do. So, she remained silent as he took his leave. Althyn drew the coverlet over her flushed skin and closed her eyes. She tried to imagine Tolston with her, but her mind kept showing her Lainious, and he bore that same lustful expression he'd had when he hovered over her before the kiss.

ANTHIS EMBRACED ALTHYN and pressed a kiss to each of her cheeks. He looked terribly sad that she was leaving, but he said nothing to sway her to stay. He knew better. "Return safely," he muttered, and looked out over the dock to the ship that had once been his brother's. "I will look for your flag flying upon the mast each night until you come to the temple."

"And you will see it soon enough," she said with a comforting pat to his shoulder. "I will have what I want and bring him here to sit by my side as I rule."

"You have your father's will." Anthis backed away and nodded.

Althyn turned and sauntered along the island's largest dock. The white dress she wore fluttered in the cool breeze coming in off the sea. There was no crew aboard the ship save her one servant. He stood by the gangplank with an unreadable expression. She bypassed him and took her place at the ship's fore. Once Lainious had drawn in the anchor and lines holding them there, Althyn began to sing. She called for the wind to fill the sails, and it did as she wished. She lured the waves to push her ship's bow away and into the sea, and they obeyed. Froth churned alongside the wood planks that made up her vessel. The ship picked up speed, moving at an unnaturally quick pace.

When they were far from sight of the temple and the island, Althyn went silent. She looked over her shoulder to see Lainious standing by the cabin door, mending nets without looking down at his work. He watched her, his lips pressed together tightly, his blue eyes fierce. She half expected him to reprimand her for this journey, to order her to turn back. Part of her *wanted* him to do that. But he did not. He simply stared and waited.

She turned back to the horizon and watched the water change to a deeper blue the farther they journeyed. The sun began to dip toward the line of ocean and the clouds in the sky changed colors to reds and pinks, blending and becoming more vibrant the more the sun slipped away. A shiver ran through her. She knew Othia had somehow touched her, and the god's essence had become a part of her, if only slightly. When the sun had finally parted for the day, and the night sky was filled with stars, she felt Lainious come to stand at her side.

"Are you hungry?"

She nodded.

"I'll prepare a meal for you." He started to leave until she turned her face to look at him. Lainious was dressed in his usual attire, dark pants and sandals, with nothing else. He looked sad, distant, but he hesitated and shot her a smile. "Wine too?"

"Yes, that sounds good."

She followed him with her eyes as he made his way to the cabin. He was as pleasing as ever to look upon, maybe more since the kiss. She chewed at her lower lip and wondered what would happen when she found Tolston. Although she felt drawn to the mate she had chosen, her servant presented a different course of action. She could have him now, anytime she wanted him. But if she took Lainious to her bed and claimed him as she had done with Tolston, would the same fate befall her a second time? Would Lainious then renounce his loyalty and forsake her? She sighed and followed the way he had gone to take her night meal in the room.

In the short hall she found him about to bring a tray of fruit, cheese, and meats to her bed. He paused there until she entered, and inside, she sat upon the bed to watch as he brought forth the meal. After he set the tray beside her, he sat on the floor and watched as she ate.

"You look like you want to tell me something." She sipped at the wine, finding it sweet.

He blinked and half smiled. "I have said all I wish to say to you already."

She nibbled at a roll of bread. "What's to become of me now?"

"I don't know what you mean, Althyn. You rule the Othian temple. You have people to follow and worship you. You are a great queen and, in the eyes of many, you are the temple's priestess. I suppose there is more you might wish to do, to discover and claim as your own."

She quirked an eyebrow. "You wish me to claim you."

His lips tensed. "I am yours."

"Yes, you are that." She ate a little more, thinking over what might happen in Truias. The closer they got to the port town, the more she worried that seeking out Tolston was a mistake. Her mother had never left the island in search of her father. And as far as she knew, her mother had only ever wanted one mate. *Maybe it's different for me,* she reasoned. *Because I am not fully mer.*

"Are you done?" Lainious asked, nodding toward the tray.

"Yes, yes, take it away. I'll sleep now." She scooted back on the bed and pretended not to take notice of him as he cleaned up and carried away what she hadn't eaten. She picked at her nails, stole glances at the looking glass every so often, but after he left her room, she waited impatiently for him to return and warm her bed.

Well past the time the three moons would have joined as one, Althyn climbed out of her empty bed and crept up to the deck. There she saw Lainious, a short sword in his right hand as he danced like a bloodthirsty warrior, parrying and stabbing at a phantom foe. His muscles rippled in the blue moonlight, his mouth in a snarl as he sliced and dodged. She leaned against the cabin wall and watched, silent, so that he wouldn't know she was there.

He practiced this fight until his skin glistened with sweat and his chest heaved for breath. Weary, he set his blade down among the pile of nets and turned his back to her while he kicked off his shoes and stripped away his pants. Naked, he strode to the prow of the ship, which still rushed forth without her musical guidance. The wind picked up his dark hair and blew it all about. He raised his arms at his sides as if he would catch the air and fly away.

Curious, Althyn made her way to him, as soundlessly as possible. When she stood at his back, she said, "Come to bed now. The hour is late."

He flinched and dropped his arms to his sides. "I'll sleep up here so I don't disturb you." He didn't turn to look at her, and she wanted him to. Instead, he stepped to the very edge of the bow and looked down at the mermaid figurehead the ship bore. It was at that moment that Althyn realized the carving was likely a depiction of her mother.

"The bed is cold. Warm it for me." She set her hand on his bare skin and found it chilled from standing there in the nude, sweating.

He trembled and shook his head. "You've made your choice. Only one man should lie with you. It's the way of things."

Her hand fell away and she moved to stand at his side. Her loose hair whipped behind her shoulders to dance in the breeze. "I say what the way of things will be, and I say you warm my bed."

"No."

His defiant answer irked her. She wouldn't stoop to begging. Dragging him there would be much more demeaning to her. Althyn set her hands on the wood handrail and sighed. "Fine. Then neither of us shall sleep."

Chapter Twenty-Four
Return to Truias

SEAGULLS FLEW IN graceful arcs over the bustling port town. Althyn was tired, but she refused to show her fatigue. The time had come to reclaim the mate she had chosen. She would make him come back to the temple with her if she had to tie him up and drag him onto her ship. She held her long sword in one hand, the leather clad tip resting on the boat's deck. She breathed in the scent of the place; fish, baking bread, the stifling odor of people and civilization.

"I suggest you take a horse this time," Lainious said. He had darkness under his eyes and his countenance had not improved over the sleepless night. "Although, if you need to leave quickly, you have the means without one."

"A horse." She grinned. "Yes, that's what I will do. Make a grand entrance atop a great, white horse." Her uncle had told her fairytales of princes who rescued women. They always rode white horses. Since she was a queen of the underworld, she thought she ought to have a white horse, too. She slipped her scabbard's belt over her shoulder and started down the plank, her footsteps light.

Lainious remained on the ship without her asking him to stay. She didn't look back at him, her instincts kicking in. No, she needed to get Tolston. He was the mate she wanted. She made her way along the line of merchants, drawing attention from everyone she passed. Eventually, she reached a livestock trader. The older man was bearded and bent.

"I need a horse," she announced, and took out a purse of coins. "A white one."

The merchant eyed her with a toothy grin. "I have just the animal for you." He waved her forth and they walked past a gated area of goats, and then another with caged birds. In the rear of the building his business occupied, they came upon a small herd of horses.

"There." He pointed out a speckled gray mare that busied herself eating hay from a pile.

"White," Althyn said. "I want a *white* one."

The man scratched at his chin for a moment. "Are you an experienced rider?"

She set a hand on her hip. "I want a white horse, the bigger the better. What difference does it make if I'm experienced? I have gold to spend."

"All right." His grin faded. "I have one white horse...a stallion. He's not tame."

"Bring him here then."

The man nodded, looking skeptical. He opened the gate and trudged through the clods of dirt and hay until he reached a post with bridles. He took up one and went into the makeshift wooden building. A few brown horses trotted out. Althyn tapped her foot, impatient.

A horrible, feral scream broke out from the building. She heard the man shout a few words she didn't understand. The beast he had spoken of reared as it left the building, a rope tied to the bridle it wore. Its eyes flashed white and blue with fury.

"Yes! That one! He is mine." She stepped up to the fence, excited. When the horse saw her, it neighed and tossed its mane.

The man named his price, but she was in no mood to bargain. She thrust the coin purse into his hand and reached for the horse's rein, snatching it away. She led the animal along the fence to the gate, opened it, and then the two left the market. She supposed she ought to try to ride the horse by the time they had reached the edge of the port town. The road to the lord's holdings was long and winding. She had walked it last time, but Lainious was right. She should make a grand entrance.

Gripping the leather reins tight, she attempted to climb upon the horse's bare back. A shiver ran over the stallion's coat. He glanced back at her and bared his teeth in warning. "Enough of that," she said. "You belong to me. You'll do as I say."

She gave the horse's sides a kick as she had seen men do at the lord's keep the last time she'd come to Truias. The animal nickered and half bucked, half started into a trot. Satisfied, even though riding atop the creature made for an uncomfortable, bumping journey, she thought she made a beautiful sight as she rode along the merchant strip and then onto the road leading to the keep. The gates there were wide open, one guard posted and did not act worried about whether she entered or not. He raised a hand to her and frowned, as if he recognized her.

She reached out with her mind and listened for the deep sound of Tolston's masculine voice. She heard nothing of him, felt no sign. At the fountain where she had paused on her prior visit, she slipped down from the horse's back and stomped through the courtyard, remembering the way. There, the guards did take notice of her. One managed to grasp her arm and pull her aside to question her.

"Where are you going, lady?"

His gruff hold irritated her, but his voice was familiar. She faced him and grinned. "Oh, it's you."

He smiled, but she saw no kindness in the expression, not like before. The milder disposition and willingness to help was gone. It was Tolston's brother, Doran. He looked different somehow, broken. "You are the cause of this."

"Cause of what?"

He sneered and nodded at the courtyard and the hold. "The change in my brother. Certainly he was a cruel man before you, but now..." He shook his head and stared at the hall behind her. "Now he is pure evil, a man bent on dominating everything in his path."

She blew out a hissing sigh. "And you think I have something to do with that? Bedding me didn't change him. He was that way before. You simply didn't see it. Now it's obvious." She shook free of his grip. "Where is he? I wish to take him back to the temple with me where he belongs."

"Temple? What temple?"

"I have taken the Othian Temple in Nemba. It's mine. Tolston will return there now and stand at my side."

Doran laughed sarcastically. "It is you who doesn't see him for what he is. My brother will never follow the will of a woman, no matter how powerful or beautiful. He's misled you if you believe that."

"Then I will *take* him. It is not a choice to follow or not."

"You're not even human." He held up his hands at her, as if letting her go on was releasing him of some debt. "Go and kill him. Spare this port town his cruelty. He is a worse tyrant than the lord that went before him. Already my brother has killed the heirs of Truias. He sits as ruler, a lie of his own making that everyone believes unless they long for a quick death."

"I have no wish to kill him." She scoffed and strode away to find her mate.

"He may well kill *you,* if you're not careful..." Doran's words drifted along the cool air as she entered the keep, speaking of her past and what could befall her soon. If he did, she will have gone the way of her mother. The parallel wasn't lost on Althyn as she hurried along.

Up stone stairs that led to the room she had killed off the lord, she went her way, determined, but a little distressed in the changes that had occurred since she'd been here last. Streaks of dried blood were patterned on the stone walls and even across fine tapestries, marring their beauty. She had not done that damage.

At the carved doors, she paused, thinking. She heard his voice on the other side of the door, deep and commanding, a little irritated as he shouted at whoever was in the room with him. Her body shivered uncontrollably. Althyn reached for her sword and drew the awkward blade. Holding the weapon calmed her, helped her prepare.

Clenching her teeth, she said, "Tolston!" and pushed the door open.

There stood her mate, two bare women in the bed before him, their bodies curled together as they listened to him talk. He turned his head to see who had interrupted his tirade and frowned. "You."

"Yes, me. Come home now. You belong to me."

He took a step toward her, his frown turning into a lascivious grin. "Why should I? I have all that I need here, woman. Whores and chambermaids to warm my bed at all hours of the day or night. A throne to sit upon, a town and its holdings to rule over. My thanks to you for dispatching the lord. After seeing you take that which could not be taken, I realized that I could have what I've always wanted. There was no one to stop me." He swept his hand before himself, puffing out his chest. "And I have taken it. All of it."

"You belong to me," she repeated. "You're mine. *Mine!* You'll do as I say."

He choked on his laughter. "Or what? You'll poke me with that oversized sword? I daresay you still don't know how to properly wield it. Our lessons were harried and, although you wielded my blade well at our last tryst, that one is far above your skill level to be useful."

She came charging at him then, her anger bubbling to the surface. The women on the bed were laughing at her, as if she were ridiculous, not a priestess of Othia, not a woman that mattered to Tolston, not important at all. When she was a few feet from her mate, she swung the sword. It arced downward as she pivoted and sliced hard into the bedcovers and overstuffed mattress. The women screamed, suddenly fearful. They scrambled to the opposite side of the bed and rushed to make a quick escape.

Tolston snapped Althyn to his chest with two rough hands. He held her backside pressed to his body. "Oh, look now what you've done. Scared my little pretties away."

The women streaked through the still open door and down the hall.

"You'll take no other to your bed but me."

He laughed in her ear, his breath warm and lusty. "Why not? Why should I save anything for you? Do you still keep that manslave of yours?"

"Lainious is mine. It's none of your affair that I keep him."

He nipped at her earlobe and she thought she would melt in his arms. Her anger was certainly melting away. "Woman, enjoy your little manslave, for that's the only cock you'll find in your fanciful temple henhouse. I'm not going back there to be ruled by you and your foolish whims. I know your kind. Selfish, spoiled, dangerous. I know what you are because we are one in the same."

She exhaled when he sucked her earlobe into his mouth and tongued it. "Come back with me." It sounded like she was begging now.

"Stay here with me," he said when he released her. "I'll tie you down in this bed every night and do you like I did in my bed chamber on the floor. You like it like that. I know you do. And when you're bad, I'll make you watch me as I take the other ones. I'll force you to watch. In time, you'll like that too, won't you?"

She shook her head, disgusted.

"No? Not what you expected?" He bit into her shoulder and then kissed away the small hurt his teeth had caused. "What do you think? That people like us settle in and raise half-breed children? That we stop craving power and riches and decide to stay in one place to wile our lives away and die of old age?"

Had she thought that? Had she wanted that from him? Now that he'd said as much, she realized she did want it, more than anything. She didn't know why or how, but she truly needed that kind of stability in her life...and yet she knew. Althyn knew he was right. She could no more settle down as he had described than a butterfly could stop flitting from flower to flower. To stop would be certain death. A slow death of stale days spent doing nothing. No, she was not that. Althyn was a force that kept roiling as it moved over the land or sea. She was feral and wild, and even as much as she wanted to be what she was not, she realized at that moment that she could never truly be happy.

She dropped her sword. It clattered to the tile floor, the sound echoing. She felt cold, icy and cruel. Tolston's tongue on her neck was replaced by metal, which was just as cold and unyielding as she. Its sharp edge bit into her skin and she felt complete. Her life was about to end at the hands of the mate she had chosen.

She sighed. "Do it. If this is what you truly want."

"There isn't enough room in this world for two like us, Althyn. You must know that. We would always be at odds, and although I enjoyed our romps, it's never enough for me. I'll want others. I've always been like that."

He walked forth, forcing her to step in time until she was pressed between him and the edge of the bed. "Maybe one more time. There's something about you..." His other hand slid along her waist and higher until he brushed her breast and nipple. "Something I can't quite place. I want to be with you...yet I don't. I can't understand it. I don't want to."

"Let her go."

The three words that filled the tense silence shocked Althyn. It was Lainious. She turned her head though the dagger Tolston had to her throat bit deeper into her skin. Her servant stood there with his short sword in hand and a determined scowl on his face. His blue eyes glittered with malice. He wore only his dark pants and sandals as he had the first day she'd seen him.

"Are you the hero?" Tolston asked with a sardonic chuckle. "You? Am I to believe you would want to save this wench from me?" He thrust Althyn away from him. She fell onto the ruined bed in a heap and set her hand to her bleeding neck.

"She is *my* lady," Lainious said, sounding much braver than Althyn thought possible.

Tolston bent and retrieved her long sword. He held it aloft in one fist, and Althyn glared when she rolled on her back to see what would happen. She wished the sword would burn hot and make him drop it. He didn't deserve to hold her weapon; she hadn't given him her permission. Even as she thought it, the blade began to glow. From tip to hilt it became fiery red until Tolston released it. He glanced at his hand and grimaced. "Sorceress. You'll pay for that."

"You'll pay, "Lainious challenged. He came forward, his steps slow, steady. Althyn's chest swelled for a moment at his courage. He had come to defend her. He had come to save her from the ill fate she had chosen.

He will fail, she thought.

Chapter Twenty-Five
The Dragon

ALTYHYN CALLED THE water in the air to her. She willed it to make a mist, and it did so, filling the room with a gray haze until Lainious and Tolston were but two shadows approaching one another, each disregarding her magic. Tolston lunged first, knocking the blade from Lainious's hand in one strong swipe of his fist. He swung again, the dagger he had used at her neck shining as it sought a place to bury itself. Her servant dodged and kicked his sword to one side, chasing after it and avoiding his attacker.

She pushed herself to stand. They would obey her. Even Tolston would bow to her and stop his ridiculous taunts to subdue her will. He belonged to her. She would claim him and take him back to the temple. Whatever the cost.

Lainious picked up his blade. He swiped as the mist thickened and he slashed Tolston's leg. But his blow met a thick leather boot. Althyn sucked in a breath. She didn't want Tolston harmed, neither of them.

When her mate landed a blow to Lainious's temple, felling him completely, she covered her mouth to hide her startled cry. It came out as a whimper.

Tolston hovered over his victim and laughed. His voice boomed in the room, and it was clear to her that he had succumbed to the same madness her father had suffered. Even if he had been vile before he had mated with her, Doran was right. Tolston had changed into something far worse. He continued to laugh, harder and louder, until his breathing became hitched.

"Enough," Althyn said, the mists receding.

"En-ough. Wh-what, woman? Enough that I beat your manslave down? You have no power over my heart." He laughed a little while longer before he approached her. "You never did."

"I carry your child," she blurted.

He shot back a reply. "What of it? There are many wombs I've filled with my seed. Yours is nothing better or worse. Another bastard to work the fields or fish the sea in my empire. And that's what it will be...an empire." He sucked in an awed breath. "Oh yes. An empire. I'll have the troops go to the next towns. Conquer them. Have them swear their loyalty and tithes to me. Then further."

She raised her hand and slapped his face. The resounding crack pulled him out of his reverie.

"I'll show you," he growled. His fist raised and he slung it full force. Bone and strength smashed into her cheek and eye, blinding her with pain. She stumbled, hands out, as she tried to find purchase to steady herself. Another blow, this time to her stomach. The pain made her double over, clutching the place he had injured.

The child, she thought. It was the first time she had worried over the life of another since her mother's passing.

Tolston started to laugh once more. "That's it," he said between guffaws. "You need a beating to learn your place."

He kicked her onto her side. Anger wouldn't come to save her this time. There was too much pain. It didn't allow her to concentrate. She would have liked to have made him suffer for what he'd done, but she felt helpless, trapped by the ripple of shivers that quaked through her body. Hot warmth ran down her inner thigh. *Blood. I'm bleeding.*

She looked to where Lainious had fallen, wanting to catch a glimpse of him before Tolston laid into her again. But he wasn't there. She squinted, thinking her mind was playing tricks on her, certain she remembered where he had fallen.

A strangled cry of fury made her lift her chin to see the shining blade of her long sword come crashing down into Tolston's shoulder. It sank into the meat of him, raised, than swept again sideways. She pinched her eyes shut and turned away. A gaping wound filled her heart. A dreadful emptiness.

She heard the squish of metal entering flesh several more times. It reminded her of the night she had killed her father, of the bloody, wet sound of the axe sinking and severing, chopping and ending.

Trembling, warm fingers settled on her cheeks soon after. "Mistress." The fingers ran up and down her face, gentle, kind. "Althyn. Are you injured?"

She shook her head no and let Lainious lift her to the bed. He pulled a coverlet around her shoulders. His fingers tested the wound on her throat.

"He would have killed you," he whispered. "I couldn't let him do that."

"I don't need your help." Her voice came out in a squeak. "I don't need you..."

His lips pressed to her forehead. "No, mistress. But I need you. More than life itself, I need you."

"I think he's killed my child."

Lainious curved his arms around her shoulders and held her while she wept. She didn't understand the wave of emotion that crashed into her at that moment. She was filled with sorrow, with a sense of loss for something that might have been. She had lost her mate, and though he was a terrible villain of a man that she doubted had felt anything but lust for her, he had been a challenge. He had made her want for more.

"Can we go back to the temple now?" Lainious asked.

She slipped her arms around him and held tight. Althyn breathed in his scent and felt the strange lavender mist of her magic surround them. As the child within her passed away, her allure increased. Lainious would not know the free will he had exerted this day. He would become her slave once more, lost in her gaze, unable to resist her commands no matter how inane they might be.

She buried her face in his chest and sobbed for a time. Everything had been ruined.

"Yes, we can go. But I want his weapons. Every single blade he took from another and placed on his wall. I want them. I will have them by my bed to remind me what a fool I've been. My body will not rule my heart or mind ever again."

She felt his mouth caress her cheek, then dip down to run warm lips against hers. "I love you," he said, breathless. "I feel the change coming over me. Soon it will be like it was. But I loved you then, Althyn. I loved you when I saw you stand on that dock and look up at the ship where your father kept me prisoner. I loved you when I came to your bedside and made you sandals. I may not understand the hold you have over me, but there is more to what I feel than that hold. So much more."

She pushed closer until his mouth covered hers and his lips nipped and tasted. His body felt good, well muscled, but not overly heavy. Lean and used to work. Sinuous and able to hold her when she needed comfort most. Not that she would ever admit such a thing.

Perhaps this was love, this strange emotion that did not strive to hurt or control. He took nothing from her, wanted only to be at her side and serve. *Yes, this is love like my mother and I shared. We never wished each other ill. We only wished to live with all our hearts and souls.*

She broke their kiss and opened her mouth to confess to her servant that, indeed, she did love him.

A scream made her snap her mouth shut. One of the women had returned with armed guards. Apparently, the sight of Tolston's severed head was enough to send the wench into hysterics. Not that Althyn would look directly at what had become of her mate.

"I want the weapons," she reminded Lainious. "And my white horse in the courtyard. I'll distract these men, and you'll fetch what I want for me. You'll gather it all up and bring it to my ship. Only then will we set sail for the temple."

"Anything you wish, I will do."

She reached for the bindings of her dress and unlaced them. The outer layer slowly slithered down her body. The chemise came next, crumpling to the ground. She did not dare look down at the blood trailing over her inner thigh to the floor. Her anger answered now, and her desire to keep her servant safe took over. She knew there were too many men for a gryphon. Far too many. This time she needed to be something more fearsome. Something huge and undefeatable. She held her hands before her to warn them silently that they must halt their approach.

But they did not. The guards lurched forth, clearly unsure of why a woman stood before them naked and near the body of their fallen leader.

The shift began, manipulating her innards, her muscles, her bones. She envisioned the worst creature on the planet, a reptilian beast her uncle spoke of in his winding tales. A scaled animal with great purple wings and breastplates like the strongest armor. Her body elongated, changed, grew until black claws gouged the tile and wide, batlike wings brushed the high ceiling. Lainious ran from her, the long sword in his hands. He passed the men who had come to challenge her. Some of them began to step back in a silent retreat.

Her stomach gurgled with hunger. Heat shot up her long neck. Althyn opened her toothy maw and belched out a stream of liquid fire. Men shrieked and scattered. But not all were fortunate enough to escape. The scent of burning skin and hair rent the air. The room, which had been so grand and large moments before, now felt cramped. She snapped at the men she'd felled and gobbled them up, swallowing their bodies in chunks.

Her tail lashed from side to side, crushing anything in its path. Glass tinkled. Fabric ripped. Althyn dropped her forelegs to the ground and let out a grating roar. She snapped at the few guards remaining and then stomped right over them into the hall, crushing their bodies like so many useless insects.

Fury raged inside her reptilian body. She had become the dragon of her uncle's stories, a fire-breathing monster that could not be taken down or destroyed. She braced herself and slung her body against the hall. Stones and mortar came crashing down. She smashed into the wall a second time and broke through, creating an exit large enough to leave this place.

Her body no longer ached from Tolston's beating. It felt thick and strong. Her heart pounded in her chest. She crashed through the courtyard and saw the white stallion she'd bought earlier as it reared. Her black tongue flicked out to taste the air. Although she'd feasted on the guards, she longed for more, for meat, red, ripe, raw flesh to fill her stomach and sate the emptiness.

No, the emptiness had not left her in this form. She felt it straining to tear her apart, to make her claim another mate and soil her body a second time. She spread the leathery wings she bore and flapped them. Air whooshed. People fled in droves to escape her. She jumped and caught a breeze, climbed up and over the hold.

Let it all burn, she though, soaring higher. The dragon circled and Althyn did something strange. She let the beast that she had become take over the shape of her changed body. She pushed back her soul, her thoughts and will. She felt like a watcher inside the dragon's mind as it arced mid-air and dove, spurting its heated fury down on all the homes and fields, destroying livestock, people, everything it touched.

At that moment, it didn't hurt to be a dragon. It didn't bespeak loneliness, even though she longed to be part of something greater. Maybe she could live out her years in this shape. It was not an unpleasant end. Even as she blocked out all that had happened, her womb clenched and she felt the tiny spot of death inside her as it left her body, a speck of magic dying out and falling to the ground far below. Lost. Alone. Never to live.

And she felt they were the same. Only she had survived long enough to know that she never should have been born.

Chapter Twenty-Six
Lainious

FOR THREE MOON cycles she wandered the skies and destroyed all life that she came across. Althyn was becoming the dragon she had shifted into, and each day that passed into oblivion erased a little more of what she had been before the change. When she returned to the place it had begun, the ship that had been hers was no longer in the port by the ruined town of Truias. She had expected the vessel to be there, although she wasn't clear why. Althyn wanted to find that ship—needed to find it. She thought maybe the ship would end the emptiness she felt. The hunger. The dull pain of being the only thing like her. The dragon wanted to find the ship, too. For there were no other dragons. None that she could find in her wanderings thus far. There were no other creatures like Althyn in her true form either. Becoming this thing had not changed that fact, only worsened its truth. And the dragon knew the same pain Althyn had lived with for so long. So, she followed the bluest moon across the sea, seeking out that ship.

A name drifted in her thoughts. His name. She let herself remember him. *Lainious.* He had left her, but she would find him again. He would ease the emptiness, hold her if she craved his touch. The dragon she had become resisted this line of thinking. It could not understand that finding the ship would be finding him. The dragon would eat the man. Swallow him down like so many before. Men were not special or needed. They were food. Sustenance so that she could continue her hunt. The hunt for the ship...

Lainious. The hunt for Lainious, she thought.

She crossed over a small island that was little more than cliffs and sharp edges, but there on the highest peak, she saw a white gryphon perched, watching over the waves below. This sight brought a stab of pain. She remembered her white sister, a gryphon lost by its mother. Althyn had been lost by her mother, as well. Her soul pushed forth, asserting her will and escaping the strange living hiding place she had sought refuge within. She had been the old Althyn who hadn't the courage to stand and fight. Scared. Hiding. Unable to face the challenge of her father's dominance, of what it might mean to actually love another being. She had loved her mother. Her mother had died. To love another being, that would put her at risk to be hurt again.

Lainious.

Mid-flight she shook her great, scaled head to rid her mind of the beast's instincts. She was Althyn, a mixed breed that men might think was a beautiful, enchanting woman. She was Althyn, the temple priestess of Othia. She was Althyn, destroyer of Truias, avenger of her mother's cruel, untimely death. A powerful sorceress, ruler of the watery underworld if she chose to lay claim to it. And she would go home now, home to the servant so enamored of her. Home to his arms and the comfort she felt when he slept in her bed. But she could not love him or take him as her mate. She knew what would happen if she did so. It would end in disaster as it had with Tolston, as it had with her mother and father. Her kind could not, should not love. It was simply too dangerous.

The stars glittered like countless diamonds. She longed to hold each one in her claw-tipped fingers, to clutch them and own them. The dragon's greed spilled over into her thoughts, blending, mingling. Greed made sense. She would have what she wanted. She would claim every Othian Temple until they all fell under her rule. She would find every sparkling gem ever cut into a pleasing shape by a jewel vendor and make them hers, take them if she had to. Every weapon that an enemy raised against her, she would claim and add to her collection.

The crisp sea air chilled her cold, reptilian blood. She needed the sun to rise across the sky and heat up her body. The cold made her lethargic. Nevertheless, she pressed on, flying farther over the sea than she had dared in her prior searches. She sniffed at the air, flicking out her forked tongue to taste the familiar scent of the waves that shimmered beneath her. The salty flavor beckoned the mermaid inside her. She was too many things at once, and it was not easy to reconcile the desires of every facet of her soul. She was like a jewel with many sides, each with its unique shape, each sparkling in a certain color when the light caught it just right.

Her serpentine eyes sought out the shadows that swam beneath the water, and she knew what they were. Silhouettes that, to a sailor's eyes, would appear to be large fish. Nothing was as it seemed. She knew the mer for what they were; a part of her.

She pressed on, gliding on the high rifts of cool air sent up by the water below. Then, the island came into view, a shadowy image on the horizon with torches alight upon its surface. It was like the sky to her, darker though, the dancing flames replacing the stars. The dragon searched the docks, eyes scanning each fisher's ship for the one vessel that she had sought. As if her nightmare of solitude had ended, she found it. She saw her white gryphon flag flapping in the wind, and the familiar masts and shape of the ship that had carried her away from her mother's island.

Lainious is here. The realization sent ripples of excitement through her dragon form, making the beast's scaled hackles rise as if it were preparing for battle. Claws clicked together, and its tail swirled from side to side to reveal how anxious it was not to be alone.

Althyn bowed her wings and reached out her long, muscular legs as she slowed and lowered to the beach. Her wings stirred up a cloud of sand. She closed her eyes and willed her body to diminish, to change into the shape she had been born to walk in. It hurt to shift after so many days of being trapped in that form. When she emerged, much smaller and less of a beast in appearance, she fell to her knees. Althyn stared at her hands, which were partly pushed into the sand. She was pale and naked, cold and tired. The moonlight made the world appear gray-blue. She lowered herself to the sand and rolled over onto her back. There were still so many unanswered questions, so many more places to discover and conquer, but she was tired, and now that she had taken her true form, she felt the strange effects of the poison that cursed priest had stabbed into her. Her fingers and toes were numb. Her legs tingled. For three months she had not drank the remedy Lainious knew to make her. She wondered, if she lay here long enough, if she would die from the effects.

"Lainious," she said, her voice gentle and soft. She closed her eyes and envisioned him, strong and so submissive, but not when she had needed him most. No, he had defied her definition of him. He had saved her from herself. But never could she thank him, or tell him the truth. She needed to be strong, to be in control, to hold all the power over what she had taken as hers. And he was hers. In every way...*almost* every way.

She sang to the three moons of Radaeh, and to the sea, paces from her feet. Her sweet voice rose up over the village like an eerie lure, calling out to the man she desired, to her servant, if he was indeed in the temple. She sang as her mother used to do, with painful longing, with the emptiness in her heart bared and set upon the world in a haunting melody. She sang and sang until she heard the dull sound of footsteps approaching. It could be one of the villagers. It could be her cousin, Sherak, coming up from the sea to offer her solace. But she opened her eyes and looked up at the man she had sung for, and found him staring down at her in awe.

"Althyn, you have come home." He knelt at her side and ran his shaking fingers over her face, down her cheek, across her lips. "You're alive."

She smiled up at him. "Of course. You fool. No one can stop me."

He smiled too, looking both startled and at ease. "I have missed you."

She wanted to confess the truth in her heart, that she had missed him, too. That she needed him like she needed to eat or drink when she had not had either for days. She needed him like the dragon had needed to lie in the sun and soak up its warmth. But to admit such would be to admit her weakness. It would not make her powerful.

"Help me up. I want to sleep in my own bed this night."

He nodded and pushed his arm behind her bare shoulders, lifting her to stand. Her legs were weak, shaky. She couldn't feel much from the waist down now.

"And when we are back in my room, you must make me your potion."

"Of course, Althyn." His face lined with worry, his eyes taking in her nakedness with a calculating sweep. "I can't understand how you're not worse off than this, after three moon passes of not drinking the antidote."

"I was not myself," she said. "I remained as I was after I left you in Truias. Perhaps to a dragon, the sting of scorpion venom is nothing."

He nodded and supported her as they walked along the winding path, up and up to the safety of the temple above the village. She breathed in every sweet scent about this island, the white flowers like honey, the thick vines giving off their own earthy scent, the clean, soapy smell of Lainious's skin and pants. She did feel that she was home, at last. She was not alone. She had him to take care of her until she was well enough to strike out again on another adventure.

"Tolston's weapons..." she began.

"All are hung in your room as you had requested. I've left a place for the Othian Dagger once it is recovered, and the hooks for your axe remain empty."

"And my horse?"

"In the temple stables, although I must say, he is an unruly beast that fears riding in a ship at sea. I had to sell some of the weapons to hire a small crew, but I saved the best ones for your collection."

She laughed at this. "You are a fine servant."

His hold on her tightened briefly. He stopped, and she with him, at the arch to the hall that would lead her into the temple's labyrinth of halls. "You are a fine mistress." Lainious leaned his face to hers and kissed first her left cheek, and then her right. He paused when he faced her, and without asking, leaned in to force a hard, deep kiss to her mouth. His tongue crushed into hers. The hazy feeling of seduction swept in all around her. She wanted him. Needed him. Althyn kissed back with as much passion as he offered. She sighed in his mouth when his fingers curled up into her hair and his body pushed her back until she was held up by the stone wall and the pressure of him against her. His chest crushed into her breasts, her nipples hardening into firm nubs that tingled with need. Between her legs, her body readied to be taken by him, slicking with moisture to accept him as her mate.

My mate.

"No." She drew her mouth from his.

He kissed her neck instead, the feel of his heated affection ticklish and soothing. His hips ground against her body, revealing a thick, hard line, evidence of his arousal. That felt good against her naked center, tempting. She groaned and clung to his waist, her eyes closed, her thoughts drifting away until she had none, only the awareness of him kissing her, of him rubbing himself into her, of his fingers massaging her scalp. Of his tongue licking in slow circles. His lips. His chest. His strength.

The numbness was rising up her body as well, making it more difficult to hold herself upright. But he was holding her up with his body, with his rigid, hot, aroused body. She wanted him to take her, to pin her higher to the wall and drag away his pants to fill her up.

"You need the potion," he breathed the words into her ear, and she heard him moan as if he were in physical pain from having to stop. "You shiver even now, and I know if I let go of you, you'll fall."

"If you let go, I'll fall," she whispered. Those words meant so much more. She had fallen a long time ago, the moment she took hold of her father's axe and decided to kill him. She had been falling ever since, deeper into a dark abyss. There would never be an escape from it.

"Don't let go." She pressed a kiss to his shoulder and closed her eyes. The numbness settled throughout her body, mixing with the euphoria of wanting. Lainious placed his arm behind her knees and lifted her up. She felt the sway of her body, so distant. She breathed in Lainious. Her awareness waned until she felt the softness of blankets beneath her body and heard the clink-clink of him stirring.

Lainious's weight shifted the bed. His hand lifted her until her lips touched the edge of the cup. Nasty bitterness filled her mouth. She tried not to gag as she swallowed it down.

"Maybe once each day now. The poison will leave your system in time." A cloth passed over her lips to wipe away the residue. "Sleep now," he said. "You are tired."

She lay back at his urging and with the help of his hands. The bed was cold. Empty save her. She heard his steps as he walked away and cleaned up what he had used to make the drink. "Stay with me," she called, as loudly as she could, but even to her ears, her voice did not hold its usual commanding tenure.

The tray he always carried made a metal tapping sound as he set things atop it. Footsteps. The door opening, then shutting. Althyn was alone. She breathed in and out, some breaths strained. As she lay there, half aware, she felt the numbness receding. It left a sweeping sensation of needles pricking her skin in its wake as it made its way back down her body along her chest, past her waist, her thighs, her calves, until it vanished at her toes.

She rolled onto her side and reached for the pillow, tugging it close to her body.

Sleep pulled her down into the darkness.

Much later, opening her eyes, she saw that the stained glass window had been repaired. It had a new design set into it, a fair-skinned woman whose body was shaped like a fish from the waist down. She held her arm over her breasts in modesty. Her cut glass eyes were green. Her lips were a bright cherry color. Lainious had done that. He'd had them remake the window in her image.

Althyn settled backwards and felt the heat of his hard body behind her. His arm came about her waist as he pulled her in closer. Still asleep, he murmured her name. She reached down and traced his fingers, finally curling hers with his. His leg nudged between hers until their limbs were tangled up in a sensual knot.

She looked up at the wall of blades and weapons. There were shields, spears, daggers. She counted each, memorized every deadly shape, taking notice of the two empty places. She would have the axe and the dagger back.

Lainious yawned.

She ground backwards into him, and he moaned, pushing at her with his hips and the thickness she had remembered from the night before. Only this morning he was not clothed. His naked body and heat were hers for the taking. She decided she would hunt for the dagger and axe another day. Now it was time to enjoy what she already had.

The End

About the Author

Anastasia Rabiyah writes erotic romance, paranormal erotic romance, and dark fantasy. She often crosses genres in order to follow her muses into the darkness where they seek out destiny in all its forms. She believes in fairies, demons, angels, magic, passion, chocolate, supportive friends, e-books, and writing critique groups. Her deepest desire is to pursue her creative dreams and realize them. Every spare moment she devotes to writing for her haunting muses. She lives in Tucson, Arizona with her husband and three sons.

Visit her on the web at: www.RabiyahBooks.com

Also by Anastasia available from Purple Sword:

Demon in the Basement
Demon's Redemption
Fire and Moon
God in the Stone
In the Moon's Light
Last Kiss of the Clan Dancer
Mercer's Rebellion: Derrick 7744
Shahzar
The Skeleton's Shadow
Wolf's Gift

PURPLE SWORD PUBLICATIONS
Publisher of romantic speculative fiction.
www.PurpleSword.com

www.ingramcontent.com/pod-product-compliance
Lightning Source LLC
LaVergne TN
LVHW010057110826
845155LV00028B/379

* 9 7 8 1 9 3 6 1 6 5 4 7 6 *